Diving for the Moon

Diving
for the Moon

BY LEE F. BANTLE

MACMILLAN BOOKS FOR YOUNG READERS • NEW YORK

Text copyright © 1995 by Lee F. Bantle

Macmillan Books for Young Readers
An imprint of Simon & Schuster Children's Publishing Division
Simon & Schuster Macmillan
1230 Avenue of the Americas
New York, New York 10020

The text of this book is set in ITC Garamond Light.
Designed by Cathy Bobak
Printed and bound in USA on acid-free paper.
First edition
10 9 8 7 6 5 4 3 2 1

Library of Congress Cataloging-in-Publication Data
Bantle, Lee F.
Diving for the moon / by Lee F. Bantle.
p. cm.
Summary: The summer after they finish the sixth grade,
Bird discovers that her best friend Josh is HIV-positive.
ISBN 0-689-80004-5
[1. AIDS (Disease)—Fiction.   2. Friendship—Fiction.]   I. Title.
PZ7.B22945Di 1995   94-35207
[Fic]—dc20

ACKNOWLEDGMENTS

I would like to thank all the people who assisted with this book: My writing teachers, Catherine Woolley and Nancy Kelton; my editors, Anne Dunn and Emily Raimes; the Education Committee of the National Hemophilia Foundation; Dr. John Bantle; Dr. Elizabeth Connick; Carol Sherman, Ph.D.; Kenneth J. A. Lown, R.N.; Steven Rosen; Lynn Armentrout; Lou Ann Smith; Ken Greenwood; Holly Gates; Robyn Grant; Benette Tiffault; Robyn Millerz; Karla Melvin and Jed Mattes.

*In memory of my father, Leo Bantle,
and Nancy Cotter*

Diving for the Moon

Chapter 1

"I did it," Josh Charkey shouted as his curly, dark hair burst above the waters of Whitefish. "I did eight." Now it was Bird's turn to dive into the pinncedle cold Minnesota lake. She sucked in a deep breath, blew out, sucked in again, and dove.

Underwater, Bird swam the length of the diving platform, down one side and back the other. One length. Two. That was easy. Three. Four. At five she began to struggle, to crave oxygen. Bird did six lengths and then seven. Could she go one more? She started, but her chest felt as if it would collapse and she rushed upward. "Couldn't make it," she gasped, drinking in air.

"Try again," Josh encouraged as he hoisted himself onto the diving platform standing on its tall legs out in the lake. He clambered up three wooden steps to the upper deck, which rose above a tight-stretched trampoline. "Watch," he called. Josh leaped down onto the springy canvas, catapulted high in the air, and disappeared into the lake with a splash. Bird felt a tug on her toes before he squirted out of the water beside her.

"Are you polar bears ready for lunch?" Josh's mother called from the end of the dock. She dipped her foot into the water and jerked it out, laughing. "It's still like ice."

Bird slapped the water in front of Josh. "Race you." Ever since they were toddlers learning to swim, Josh had been faster than Bird. But this year for the first time she was an inch taller than he, and maybe she would be faster, too.

"Go!" he shouted, getting an unfair head start.

"Hey!" She dove after him. As he reached the shallows, she grabbed his leg and pulled him back.

"No fair," he said, laughing, as he latched onto

her arm so she couldn't get ahead. They struggled to shore in a tie. Bird ran for her towel as the brisk breeze painted goose pimples on her white arms and back.

Mrs. Charkey spread out a blanket at Breathtaking View, the small bluff that rose above the beach. Dotted on the hillside behind them were the ramshackle cabins of the old resort Josh's family owned.

For lunch they had tuna fish sandwiches with potato chips layered between the tuna and the butter-crust bread, homemade sweet green tomato pickles, and thick slabs of marble fudge cake. Bird crunched into her sandwich. "Yum!"

"Have another, Carolina," Josh's mother said. That was her real name—Carolina Birdsong. But Bird preferred her nickname.

When they had finished eating, Bird lay back on the blanket and stared into the open sky. Last Friday, at exactly 3:30 P.M., sixth grade had let out for the summer. That moment seemed as distant as the first day of kindergarten. Math was over. Tests were done. Three months of paradise lay ahead.

"Wanna go to the pond?" asked Josh after they

had gone inside to set their plates in the kitchen sink. The screen door banged shut behind them as Josh and Bird ran down the planked steps, across the gravel driveway, and into the woods. Mill Pond was filled with frogs, leaping and swimming, nabbing flies, and croaking to one another.

Josh and Bird slipped off their sneakers and waded in. The cool, squishy mud oozed between Bird's toes. Something soft brushed against her foot. She stopped abruptly. "Maybe we shouldn't be in here."

"Why not?"

"Bloodsuckers."

"Oh, they won't hurt you," Josh said. "Sprinkle salt on 'em. They come right off."

"What if one makes your foot bleed?" Josh had hemophilia. Sometimes when he started bleeding, it would take a long time to stop. His case was mild, so he had less risk of bleeding than someone with severe hemophilia. Bird worried about him just the same.

Josh waved away her concern. "A little cut from a bloodsucker won't hurt me. A hard fall. That's what I have to watch out for. Like the time I crashed and burned on my bike." Last summer, Josh fell on the blacktop road. His mother rushed him to the doctor in Brainerd. "They were afraid I would start bleeding inside my joints."

"But you were okay. We went fishing that night."

"The doctor injected this stuff into one of my veins. Factor VIII." Josh waded deeper into the pond. "It made my blood clot, and then I was fine." He lunged toward a bullfrog and cupped it in his hands. "Check this guy out, Bird. He looks like our long lost pet frog."

"Freckles? Is it you?" She went over and touched the frog's wet, spotted skin. "Should we put him in your sister's bed again?"

Josh hooted. "Not if we value our lives." He took the bullfrog ashore and let it go. It bounded back to the water.

Bird waded out, and the two of them plopped down in the meadow. "My mom comes up north today," Bird said as she wove her sandy brown hair into a braid.

"You think she'll say yes?"

Bird knew what he meant. They had been

discussing their plan all week. "I don't know. She's stricter than my dad."

"She has to say yes, Bird. I can't wait another year."

After leaving Josh, Bird canoed across Whitefish to the tiny cabin where she and her father stayed all summer. He was a schoolteacher and didn't have to go back to work every Monday like her mother did. Bird found him at the stove rolling fresh walleyed pike fillets in flour and frying them in butter. The hot griddle spattered and crackled, filling the kitchen with a smell somewhere between hot buttered popcorn and homemade bread baking.

Her mother was sprawled on the couch, still in a suit, having driven straight up north from her law office. A briefcase overstuffed with papers sat next to her. "How was the first week of summer?" she asked, rising and giving Bird a hug.

"Good. And as soon as you say yes, it'll be great. Can Josh and I sleep out on Ossaway Island?"

Her mother's eyebrows furrowed. "All alone?"

"We're too old to camp out in the backyard again this year, Mom."

"Hmm. Aren't there animals on that island?"

"Oh, Mothhhherrrr! It's teeny. You think bears live there?"

"They'll be all right, dear," Bird's father chimed in from across the room.

"Well, I guess so," her mother said. "It's okay with Josh's parents?"

"Yes. Yes. Yes. Call them." Bird ran to the telephone hanging on the wall and dialed the Charkeys' number. Josh answered. "She said yes." A terrific whoop exploded out of the receiver. Bird held it away from her ear so her parents could hear. Tomorrow, they would be sleeping out on Ossaway!

Chapter 2

Bird was in her bedroom late the next afternoon, packing everything she needed in a small canvas bag: swimsuit, toothbrush, soap, a deck of cards, bug spray, pocketknife, matches, marshmallows. She glanced toward the bottom drawer of her dresser. Should she take them? It hadn't happened yet. But it could at any time. What if her clothes got stained? Josh would see. The thought of it made her legs wobbly. She pulled open the dresser drawer, clutched the sanitary pads, and buried them deep in her bag.

When Bird came out of her room, she heard the rumble of thunder lumbering through the heavens. She raced out of the cabin and down the hill. Raindrops peppered the lake, pouring down faster and faster. She looked toward Ossaway, barely able to see the island through the haze. Bird stamped her foot in the downpour. Why did it have to rain!

The blustering weather raged all night, and Bird and Josh decided to camp out the next night instead. She and her father played gin rummy on the braided rug in front of the fireplace. "Mom, will you play hearts with us? We need three."

Mrs. Birdsong looked up from a stack of papers. "Maybe later. I have to finish a letter to the judge." Her mother was supposed to be taking a three-day weekend. Why, Bird wondered, did she even come to the cabin if she was just going to work?

Finally, Mrs. Birdsong snapped her briefcase shut and joined them on the floor. Bird dealt out the cards. They played three hands of hearts, and then Bird announced she was going to bed. The sooner she was asleep, the sooner it would be the day of the camp out.

* * *

Bird stood stock-still, her arms out like a scarecrow's, her eyes and mouth jammed shut. "Don't get it in my face," she said as Josh's mother spritzed her with bug spray.

"Get some sleep tonight," Mrs. Charkey called to them as they marched down the hill to the beach.

Josh's father was waiting. He gave Josh a walkie-talkie like the one he had strapped on his belt. "I'll keep this with me. If you run into trouble, I can be out there with the speedboat in a minute."

"Don't worry," Josh told him as he and Bird climbed into his wooden fishing boat. He started the five-and-a-half horsepower motor, steered the boat in an S curve, and sped full-throttle toward Ossaway Island. As the boat slipped across the lake, Bird saw two men out on the water in bright bicycle caps. It was Bill and Elliot, who had a cabin down the way. Josh changed course and aimed for them. "Going fishing?" he called over the idling motors as the boats neared each other.

"No," Elliot replied. He grabbed ahold of

Josh's boat. "Your parents invited us over for a drink."

"They didn't tell *me* they were having a party," Josh exclaimed.

Bill pointed at the camping gear in Josh's boat. "Looks as if you have plans of your own."

"We're sleeping out on Ossaway," Bird said proudly.

"Mmm. Sounds great. Elliot, why don't we ever camp out?"

Elliot raised his eyebrows. "Where would you plug in your electric blanket?" Josh and Bird laughed. "Are you two up for the summer?" Elliot asked. They nodded. "We'll have to start up our hearts competition."

"I demand a rematch," said Bill. "So *I* can shoot the moon."

"Okay," Josh said as he shoved the boats apart. "If we ever come back from the island."

Bird sat on her knees as they raced away, hanging over the bow looking for fish. As they approached Ossaway, she waited for that sound she loved—the belly of the boat scraping onto the sandy beach. At last! They were on their own.

They marched up to the clump of Norway pines above the beach and picked a spot to pitch the tent. Bird pounded in the stakes with a rock, and Josh hooked the ties into their grooves. They slipped inside, secured the center pole, and unrolled their flannel-lined sleeping bags. Josh pulled candy bars out of his duffel bag. "Do you want Kit Kat or Nestle Crunch?" he asked. He pulled out more. "Or Milky Way or Snickers?" He pulled out still more. "Or Butterfinger or Baby Ruth?"

"Josh, how many did you bring?"

"Lots." He tossed one to Bird and began eating. When he finished, he opened a second.

"Didn't you have supper?" she asked.

"Nope. We had boiled dinner. Corned beef and cabbage." He scrunched up his face. "I scraped mine into the garbage."

Outside, Josh and Bird wandered to the cattail marsh. As they waded in, minnows nibbled at their toes. Then they settled on the sandy beach, watching the first stars appear in the dusky sky. "I'll cut green sticks if you make a fire," Bird said, taking out her pocketknife. By the time she came out of the woods with two saplings, Josh had a small campfire flickering on the beach. She sharpened the sticks, and they loaded them with raw marshmallows. Josh blackened his in the flames while Bird slowly roasted hers. When they had turned the color of caramel, she sucked the crunchy blobs into her mouth, one by one, and rolled her tongue over the creamy sweetness.

After they had eaten half the bag, they went in the tent and Josh read aloud horror tales by flashlight. He made his voice low and spooky. ". . . and every summer from that day forward the drowned corpse crept ashore and dragged another girl into the depths." Bird shivered as Josh closed the book. He clicked off the light. "Bird," he whispered in the pitch-blackness. "You hear about that guy who escaped from prison?"

"What guy?"

"The one who buried his victims alive."

"You're making that up."

"I wish I were. He's somewhere up north."

"Turn the flashlight back on."

"Think we should? He might see the light."

"Josh, stop it."

"I dare you to go outside."

Bird was not going to let Josh think she was chicken. "If you come."

They slowly unzipped the mosquito net and stepped out into the cool night. *"Shhhhh!"* Josh motioned for her to follow. There was no moon. He guided them, with the beam of his flashlight, toward the center of the island. "Keep watch," he cautioned her. "If you see anyone . . ." He didn't finish the sentence.

Bird kept her eyes focused on the beam of light as they walked deeper into the woods. It flickered on something fleshy. She grabbed his arm. "Josh. What was that?"

"Where?" He moved the light back to where it had been.

"There!" she pointed. "Oh, my God!" Bird screamed, frozen in place. An arm was poking out of the earth. Someone was buried there. Bird bolted. The boat. They had to get to the boat. She heard Josh's footfalls behind her as she ran. Bird leaped in the bow, scrambled across the seats, and threw down the motor. Josh stood on the beach, panting. "Get in!" she screamed. "Hurry!"

He pointed behind him. "The tent. Our sleeping bags."

"Get in!"

Josh fell to the sand, convulsed. He couldn't talk, he was laughing so hard. Uh-oh, thought Bird. "You're great," Josh told her. He had a hard time getting the words out. "Unbelievable." More laughter. "It's a fake arm. I buried it this afternoon."

"What!" Oh, was he a sneak. She fell for his tricks every time. "You maniac!" She dropped on the sand next to him. Josh continued to tremble with laughter, and soon she was giggling, too. It was fun to be scared once you knew you were safe.

As they lay there in the coolness, long past their bedtimes, the sky began to blaze with color. Luminous bands of green and rose light streamed across the horizon. *"Oooooohhh!"* Bird marveled. "Angels are shooting off fireworks."

"It's the northern lights," Josh replied as infinite swatches of amber, pink, and white light danced through the sky. They watched the spectacle in silence for a moment.

"Josh, let's sleep on the beach tonight."

His eyes lit up. "You want to?" They got their sleeping bags and pillows and laid them on the sand next to each other. Bird squeezed mosquito repellent into her hand and then into his. They oiled their faces and zippered themselves in.

Streamers of colored light continued to soar through the heavens. The majesty of it made Bird feel wonderfully small. She and Josh stared skyward, not speaking but completely together, soaking in the wonder of this night. Alone on this little island in the middle of Whitefish Lake, the brilliant sky flashing like it never had before, it was as if they had traveled into the Milky Way. She never wanted to go back to earth.

"Bird, can I tell you something?"

"Sure. What?"

"This is a secret. I haven't told anyone."

"Okay. I won't tell a soul."

"You know how I get infusions of Factor VIII sometimes?"

"Like the time you fell off your bike?"

"Yeah. Well, one time the blood was infected."

"It was? Did it make you sick?"

"No." He was silent for a moment. "But now . . . I'm HIV-positive." He swallowed. "The AIDS virus is inside me."

Chapter 3

*Chattering finches awakened Bird the next morn-*ing. She eased out of her sleeping bag and crept down to the water. The rose light of the rising sun melted and seeped across the gentle lake.

Last night, she hadn't known what to say to Josh, except that she was glad he told her. At least she had managed to say that. But the news shocked her. And when she didn't say anything else, Josh quickly changed the subject.

Bird splashed her face with lake water once and then again and again. Her skin tingled from the bracing chill. And then, without warning, a hot flood of tears rushed down her cheeks.

Not wanting Josh to hear her crying, Bird slipped into the lake. She stroked fiercely below the surface, swimming as far as she could before coming up for a breath. She went back down, pushing harder and farther out. Bird kept going and going until the cold of the deepening water cautioned her. She made a U-turn and swam with the same strength back toward shore. She climbed out, calmed by the effort.

Josh was calling. "Bird, where are you?" She forced a smile and ran to where he lay in his sleeping bag, propped on one elbow, eating a Snickers bar. "Breakfast in bed," he told her, digging a piece of caramel out of his teeth. She dropped down on her knees next to him. "You're wet," he said as her T-shirt dripped on him.

"I took a swim."

He lifted his head off his hand. "Didn't you bring your suit?"

"Yeah. But I jumped in with my clothes on." Josh searched her face. She looked away, fighting back tears.

"Don't be sad, Bird."

She stood quickly, her back to him, not wanting him to see how upset she was. "Gonna pack up," she mumbled as she ran back to the campsite.

As she worked the stakes out of the ground, he came up behind her. "I don't have AIDS, you know. I'm not sick."

But since he had the virus, he would eventually get AIDS, wouldn't he? "When did you find out?" she asked.

"My parents told me last year. They knew for a while."

"And didn't tell?"

"Didn't want me to be worried. But I'm not. I just want to have a fun summer!" He grabbed one end of the tent and began curling it up. Bird took the other end, and they rolled it into a long cylinder, slipped it into the nylon casing, and dropped in the poles.

"Do you have to take medicine?" Bird asked.

Josh curled his upper lip in a sneer. "AZT. Three times a day."

"What's that?"

"A pill. Supposed to keep me from getting sick."

Josh lifted the tent and carried it toward the boat. Bird picked up his rolled sleeping bag, hugged it tightly to her, and followed.

After they said good-bye to the island, Josh ran her home. She stepped out onto the wood planks of the Birdsong dock. He smiled and waved as the motor idled. She wanted to say something before he left, to tell him how special he was. But the engine was chug-chug-chugging and she didn't want to embarrass him. So she just waved back. Josh shifted the motor into forward and sped away, leaving a wake of white bubbles behind.

Bird plodded up to the cabin, wanting to be near her mother even if she couldn't tell her Josh's secret. "Mom," she called, opening the front door. "I'm back." There was no answer. "Mother," she called again. She searched the cabin. "Where are you?"

She found a note on the refrigerator: "Carolina—Mom had to go back to the city. The office called." Bird's shoulders slumped. She read on. "I went to the nursery for seedlings. Glad to see the grizzly bears didn't eat you. Love, Dad." Bird stuffed the note in her pocket and ran for the farthest edge of their property. A Norway pine towered there, its skyward needles brushing the blue. Bird jumped for the first branch, hoisted herself up, and was soon three-quarters of the way to the top. She settled on a sturdy branch and hugged the trunk of the tree. The boughs were so thick that she was completely cloaked from the outside world. Here, Bird could do her best thinking.

Josh was infected with the virus that caused AIDS. How could he stand knowing it was inside him? Would AZT keep him from getting AIDS? For how long?

And what about her? She thought back to last summer when he visited his grandmother in Iowa. It was so boring, floating alone on her inner tube, hoping that a boat would go by and make some waves. What would she do all summer if Josh got sick?

The next afternoon, Bird beached her canoe at the Charkeys and headed for the cabins, passing under the old tin Melody Shores Resort sign that hung above the path. Josh's parents kept the sign even though they didn't rent out the cabins anymore.

The humid air weighed down on Bird as she climbed the hill. Josh's mother was in the main cabin alone, reading a book of poems. Josh and his father had gone to town for haircuts.

Bird tried to look as if nothing at all were different, but she couldn't get her face to cooperate. Josh's mother closed the book and leaned toward her. "What's wrong, Carolina?"

"Josh told me," Bird blurted out.

"I know. I'm glad he did."

"What's going to happen to him?"

Mrs. Charkey closed her eyes for a moment. "He's fine now. That's all we can ask."

"I get so scared."

Josh's mother reached out and pulled Bird next to her on the couch, enveloping her in her arms and resting her chin atop Bird's head. She could feel the warmth of Mrs. Charkey's ample body pressing into her, surrounding her. "I'm so glad you're Josh's friend," she whispered. "I'm so, so glad."

Bird jerked forward when she heard the screen door bang in the kitchen. She slid over just before Josh poked his head into the living room. Bird smiled with relief. She had been imagining him lying in bed, hot with fever. But here he was, standing before her, full of energy. He looked wonderful. Except for his haircut. His head was shaved down to splinters around the ears, and it was moppy long on top.

"Oh, Josh!" his mother said. "Where on earth did your father take you?"

"Pequot Lakes," he answered. "If you think I look bad, wait until you see him. It's like he got his head caught in a lawn mower." Josh's father came in with a fishing hat pulled down so low over his forehead that he had to tilt back to see.

"Henry, take off that silly hat," Mrs. Charkey commanded. He sheepishly removed it to display the most lopsided haircut Bird had ever seen. "My Lord," Mrs. Charkey exclaimed.

Josh's father began scratching his back and shoulders with both hands. "I'm covered with hair," he said. "Who wants to go swimming?"

The humidity of the day had penetrated the usually cool main cabin. Bird's skin felt sticky. "I do," she answered.

"Me, too," Josh chimed in. "Mom, come!"

"All right," Mrs. Charkey said, rising. "Who needs a beach towel?"

Josh and Bird shot off to get their suits on. He went to the white cabin that he shared with his older brother, Joe. She went to the yellow girls' cabin, still crowded with beds. When Bird was little, Josh's sisters—Lizbeth, Jane, and Lisa—all stayed there. On special occasions, Bird got to sleep over with them. But now Lizbeth was married, and Jane was away at college. She suddenly longed for them. Why did people have to go away?

In the cabin, Lisa was bent over her feet, polishing her toenails. White cotton balls were stuffed between her toes. "Oh, hi, Bird," she said. "Grab me the nail file in the bathroom, will ya? I can't walk till these dry." She laughed easily, like her mother. As Bird returned with the file, Lisa painted her big toe with a flourish. "Gorgeous, huh?"

Bird shrugged. "I guess." She wondered why anyone would want hot-pink toes. "Everyone's going swimming. You want to?"

"Sure," replied Lisa, fanning her toes. "Give me half a second."

Bird headed down the path, barefoot, in her yellow, one-piece suit, stepping gingerly over the pinecones and pebbles along the way. This early in the summer, her soles had not hardened yet. She found Josh in the equipment cabin amid the life vests and water skis. She helped him blow up rafts and drag them, along with two inner tubes, to the beach.

Joe came crashing down the hill, kicking up pinecones and sticks as he ran. "Last one in is turtle spit," he yelled in his baritone voice as he leaped off the dock. Bird and Josh were standing waist deep. They both dropped under the water in a flash.

"Beat you," Josh yelled as they stood up again.

"Did not!" Bird replied.

Josh's parents sauntered down the path, waded in, and rubbed handfuls of water across their arms and shoulders. When at last they were wet, the group formed a flotilla, bunching the rafts together, stomachs aboard and feet kicking. Mrs. Charkey sprawled in an inner tube and hooked on to the group with one leg. "Let's go out deep," she said.

"Wait for me," Lisa called, clumping down the hill on the heels of her bare feet, careful not to let her painted toes touch the path. She grabbed an inner tube and paddled out. The six of them floated past the dock, beyond the diving platform, and out into the open water of Whitefish. They kept going and going until they were halfway to the far shore. The lake was so deep. Who knew what was down there? Bird clung fast to her air mattress.

Josh dived under and resurfaced, resting just his arms on the raft. "Look! Look over there!" he shouted, pointing. "I thought I saw the giant muskie." There had long been reports that a twenty- or twenty-five pound muskellunge lived in Whitefish. Many had seen a glimpse of the fish majestically flashing its silver tail near the surface of the lake. No one had ever caught it.

"Where? I don't see anything," Lisa said.

"Right there." Josh tread water with one arm and pointed with the other. "There it is again."

"Do you see it, Henry?" Mrs. Charkey asked her husband. "Don't muskies have sharp teeth?" She pulled her legs out of the water. Slowly, she let them sink back in. Bird heaved herself forward on the mattress. Did her toes look like worms under-water?

Everyone grew quiet. Bird looked around her. Waiting. Straining to see. Suddenly, Lisa grabbed Bird's arm with a viselike grip. Both girls screamed. Lisa struggled to yank her leg out of the lake. But something was pulling it in deeper. "It's got me!" she cried.

Chapter 4

Bird tried to scramble up out of the water to get away from the muskie. It was impossible. She went topsy-turvy. So did everyone else. One after the other, they spilled into the lake, that much closer to the invader.

Underwater, Bird instinctively curled into a ball. Something slimy brushed across her legs. Help! The fish was after *her* now.

Which way could she escape? She opened her eyes. That's when she saw him. Josh was grabbing for her toes. Ah-ha! Another trick. She should have known. "There's no muskie," Bird shouted as she surfaced. "It's Josh."

A moment later, Josh's head appeared out of the water as he gasped for breath. "Why did you abandon ship?" he asked innocently, treading water and grinning as they climbed back onto the floats.

"Because someone was telling a fish story," Lisa said. They all started splashing Josh until he was forced to dive under again to escape. Then everyone settled down, enjoying the warmth of the sun as the cool water lapped against their bodies.

"I think it's time to head in," Mr. Charkey said after awhile. "I've got to go back to the city tonight." He was a building contractor and had to start work on a new house.

Bird had a sinking feeling as they paddled toward land. "Let's not get out yet," she urged Josh as the others went ashore.

"Okay. You want to do laps?" They tossed their rafts on the beach and swam out to the diving platform. "You go first," Josh said, hanging off the wooden frame that housed the trampoline.

Bird moved into starting position in front of the diagonal cross-boards that lent support to the platform's underwater legs. Determined to equal Josh's record, she dived through the opening.

She swam the length of the platform, pulled through the opening on the far side, and came back again. After four lengths, she still felt strong. She did six, seven, and then eight. Using all her willpower, she pushed herself to go one more. She burst above the surface and gulped sweet air. They could each do nine lengths on one breath now.

"We have something to tell you," Mrs. Birdsong announced the following Saturday at breakfast.

"What?" asked Bird. She spread orange marmalade on a toasted bagel half and sank her teeth in.

"There's going to be an addition to the family," said her father.

Bird practically leaped from her seat. "A dog!"

Her father chuckled. "No. Mom's pregnant."

"You are?" Bird took a swallow of grapefruit juice. After the sweet marmalade, it made her lips pucker. "*You're* having a baby?"

Bird's mother nodded. "You look surprised."

Surprised? Bird was dumbfounded. Her mother was the last person she would have guessed to be pregnant. "Are you going to quit your job?"

"Of course not."

"I don't want a nanny living with us."

"Don't worry," said her father. "No one's going to move in with us." He took a sip of steaming coffee. "Won't it be nice to have a little sister or brother?"

Bird wrinkled her nose. "I guess." A dog would be much nicer. Like Roxie, the golden retriever that lived up at Burkett Farm. "Hey, Mom, can we visit Roxie today? I haven't been to the farm yet this year."

"Hmm. We'll see."

"Please. We can pick strawberries."

"Good idea," said her father. "I'll make short-cake tonight."

"Ooh, I've had such a craving for strawberry shortcake," said her mother. "Smothered in whipped cream." She took another toasted bagel. "I'll be wearing maternity clothes soon. May as well start getting fat."

That afternoon, as Bird bent over a plant in the U-Pick-It strawberry patch at Burkett Farm, she felt something warm nuzzling her side. She turned and threw her arms around a taffy-colored dog. "Roxie! How ya been, girl?" Bird romped with the frisky retriever until the dog lit off into the woods after a rabbit.

Bird walked back to the berry patch, picked up her empty basket, and knelt down to start picking. "Can we get a puppy, Mom?" she asked. Her parents had always said no before. But it was worth one more try. "Please."

Her mother looked up from the next row. "Oh, honey. Won't we have our hands full with the new baby?"

The question jolted Bird. She had completely forgotten about the baby. Bird stared at her fingers as they yanked berries from their stems. Why did her parents suddenly want another kid? Bird picked furiously until she reached the end of a row of plants. Her quart container was full. As she stood to go and get another, her eyes focused on its contents. She gasped. Her basket was overflowing with little green and white strawberries. Not a ripe one among the bunch. Bird dropped them, spilling the berries into the dirt.

Her mother frowned. "Go on. Fill it again."

"Don't we have enough berries?" Bird cried. She turned and marched for the driveway.

"Carolina," her mother called after her. Bird didn't look back. She yanked open the car door and climbed into the stiflingly hot front seat.

Bird's mother paid Mr. Burkett and strode toward her, balancing three quarts of berries in her arms. "What's the matter with you?" she asked as she loaded the strawberries into the car. Bird was silent, pretending to be fascinated with the toolshed outside her window. Her mother climbed in front. "Are you upset about the baby?"

"How come no one asked me?" Bird demanded to know. "I'm part of this family, too."

Her mother didn't answer for a moment. Then very quietly she said, "No one asked me, either. It wasn't planned." She started the car and backed out of the driveway. "I was shocked, too," she confided to Bird. "But some things work out for the best. Even if you don't think so at first."

Bird rolled down the window, and the cool outside air rushed in. She studied her mother's body. She couldn't decide if she looked pregnant or not. "When's this baby coming?"

"I'm due on New Year's Day."

That's not till the winter, thought Bird. A long time from now.

The next day, Bird was walking up from the lake when she saw a duck fly to the roof of the cabin and land. That's funny. What's a duck doing up there? she wondered. As she got closer, Bird saw that at the edge of the roof, underneath an overhanging pine bough, the duck was making a nest. Boy, everyone is having babies, she thought.

Josh and his parents came over for supper that night. While the grown-ups had cocktails, Josh and Bird climbed a poplar tree that stood between the lake and the cabin to get a good look at the nest.

"Guess what," she whispered down to Josh,

who was seated on the branch below. "My mom's having a baby."

"Really?" Josh exclaimed.

"*Shhhhh!* Yeah. Isn't it horrible?"

"I don't know. Why?"

"A million reasons. Babies are noisy and messy. I've seen 'em throw up all over a person." Bird shook her head. "Have you ever changed a diaper, Josh?"

"No."

"Well, do you want to?"

"No way."

"And someone's always gotta watch 'em," Bird went on. "I'll be baby-sitting half my life."

"Even during summer vacation?"

"Especially during summer vacation—when the grown-ups are taking it easy."

"I'll help you baby-sit. It might be fun."

"Yeah. Just wait until we want to go fishing and we're watching the baby instead."

Just then, the duck returned to the roof with pine needles in its bill. "Look," Bird exclaimed in a whisper. "The nest is getting big."

"Wood ducks lay a lot of eggs," Josh said.

"How many?"

"Could be ten or twelve."

"Wow. At least my mother's only having one baby!"

Chapter 5

As the summer solstice arrived, a wink of light could still be seen past ten o'clock on Whitefish. Though the days were long, they seemed to slip away faster than a pond bug skittering across still water. It was easy to lose track of time, to think it was midafternoon when actually supper was on the stove.

On one of those long days in late June, Josh and Bird traipsed to the Peoria Store on a narrow dirt road about a mile from Melody Shores. A bell on the door rang as they entered, and Bird immediately spied a dozen jars of dime candy: licorice ropes, taffy, Fireballs, jawbreakers, and miniature candy bars of every kind. Josh bought a half dozen of the little bars and a bottle of grape pop. Bird got a jelly doughnut and clove-flavored gum.

As they walked back, the sun glared down. A car rumbled by and stirred dust into the air. Bird's throat felt parched. She took her doughnut out of a small white paper bag and chomped down. It was gooey and delicious. But she wasn't the only one who wanted it. Two wasps raced for the jam. Bird took off running with the doughnut stretched out in front of her. The wasps followed. "Do a quick reverse," Josh yelled. Bird screeched to a halt and charged back the way she had come. But the wasps were still in hot pursuit as she tore along the road. "Throw it down," Josh said, laughing, as she went by him.

Bird was not about to toss away a perfectly good jelly doughnut. But there was a third wasp now, and they dive-bombed her from all sides. Much as she hated to, she pitched it into the woods.

Sweaty and frustrated, Bird couldn't wait to get

into the lake. "I'm so thirsty," she said as Josh swigged his grape pop. He offered the bottle to her. Bird grabbed it and put it to her lips. Then she remembered. She handed it back without drinking.

He stared at her, his eyes intense, and then turned away. "You can't get it that way, Bird." Not knowing what to say, she just stared down at her shoes scuffing along the sandy road.

As they came up the Charkeys' driveway, Josh's mother shouted to them from the steps. "Bird! It's five o'clock. Your father's waiting." Oh no! She had lost track of the time. It was Aunt Trina's eightieth birthday. She should have been back at the cabin an hour ago to drive down to the city.

"Josh, I have to go. Bye." She brushed her hand across his shoulders.

He shrugged it off. "See ya," he said, turning his back and walking off. She didn't want to leave him this way. But she was so late. Why was she making a mess of everything today?

In the car driving to the city, Bird wondered why it was such a big deal that she wouldn't drink his stupid pop. But her annoyance gave way to a long-ing in the pit of her stomach. She would be away from Josh for three days.

On the way through Little Falls, her father stopped at Dick's Broiler for hamburgers. They ate in the car to save time. "Can you get AIDS by eat-ing someone else's food?" Bird asked as they drove.

Her father turned down the Twins game on the radio and glanced over at her. "No. You worried about that?"

"I don't know if I have to be careful around Josh." Mrs. Charkey had told Bird's parents that Josh was HIV-positive. So it was okay to talk about it with them now.

Her father lifted the root beer nestled between his legs and took a long sip. "Most people get infected by having sex with someone who has the virus." He glanced at her again. "You don't need to worry about that yet." Bird blushed. "Otherwise, the only way you could get it from Josh is if his blood got in your blood. Don't let that happen. Understand?"

"Yes."

He reached over and rubbed her shoulder. "But touching him or taking a bite of his hamburger is no problem."

So she could have had a drink of his pop. Instead she had acted as if he had leprosy. Bird sank into the bucket seat and closed her eyes. All she could see was the hurt in Josh's face as she handed the bottle back.

They got to the party just as the chocolate birthday cake was being cut into rows. Bird's mother made a champagne toast to Aunt Trina. Bird took a sip from her father's glass and had to help herself to more cake to get rid of the bitter aftertaste.

Early the next evening, as Bird watered the dusty dry plants at their home in Minneapolis, her mother arrived back from the office. Her arms were filled with bags. She set them all on the dining room table and opened one. Inside were books. Bird read the covers: *Guide to a Healthy Pregnancy, Caring for the Newborn,* and *Mother's Milk: The Case for Breast-Feeding Your Child.* Bird stared at her mother. She was going to breast-feed the baby?

Mrs. Birdsong rustled through another bag. "Now, I want your opinion. Do you like this wallpaper for the nursery?"

Bird was determined not to like it whatever it was. Her mother unrolled the sample, and Bird glanced at the kittens chasing yarn. "Oh, Mom. This one's boring."

"It is?"

"Yeah. Didn't they have any with leopards or tigers?"

"For a nursery?" Her mother looked skeptical. "We want the poor thing to sleep through the night, not scream in terror." Bird snickered. Imagine being afraid of wallpaper! "Come on," her mother said. "I like this pattern. Let's see how it looks with the carpet upstairs."

Bird shook her head. She wanted no part of all this fuss over the baby. She wandered out to the front steps and sat down. In the distance she could hear the hum of a lawn mower. The sweet smell of freshly cut grass hung heavy in the air. She wondered what Josh was doing up at Whitefish just then.

A few minutes later, Bird's mother came out and

sat down next to her. "It's nice to have you home with me." She reached over and started to massage Bird's back.

Bird couldn't remember the last time her mother had rubbed her back. She wanted to give in to the gentle stroking, but was sure she was only getting this attention because of the new baby. Bird was too smart to fall for that. She pulled away from her mother's touch. "I forgot to put my bike in the garage." She ran to the backyard, ignoring the pang of regret that shot through her.

As Bird got ready for bed that night, her father came into her room with a pamphlet from the high school where he taught. "Why don't you read this," he suggested. "About AIDS."

Bird crawled under the covers with the pamphlet. She read each question and answer. Her eyes bore down on the page when she came to one particular question: "How do people with hemophilia get AIDS?" She knew that people with hemophilia who started bleeding got an infusion of Factor VIII to make them stop. But she hadn't known that a single bottle of Factor VIII was made from the blood plasma of thousands of people. If even one of those blood donors had the virus, then the whole bottle of Factor VIII was infected. That's why, before they began screening donors and treating blood, many people with hemophilia got the AIDS virus. It was so unfair! The very thing that helped Josh to stop bleeding had made him HIV-positive.

Chapter 6

Bird and her father arrived back at Whitefish late the next evening. She helped unload groceries and went to bed. In two days, the Charkeys would throw their annual Fourth of July party at Melody Shores. Scotty Kovacs was going to launch real fireworks from the beach. Bird lay in her bunk imagining shimmers of light soaring high into the air and then crumbling into the blackness of the lake.

Bird didn't see Josh the next day because he had gone down to the city for his monthly checkup. On the afternoon of the Fourth, she found him back at Mill Pond trying to catch a garter snake. "Bird!" he

shouted when he saw her. "When did you get back?"
Good, she thought. He wasn't mad anymore.

"I brought you a present." She handed him a car scrape decal that she had gotten from the joke store. The package read "Funny Fender Bender." If you plastered the decal on a car, it looked as if the car had been in an accident.

"I've seen these," Josh exclaimed. "But I never had one."

"I wanted to get you something. 'Cause of what happened."

"You mean about the pop?" Bird nodded. "It's okay."

"But your feelings were hurt."

"So? Big deal. I've probably hurt yours."

Bird thought back to last winter. Josh and his friend Dan had led her to a mound of yellow snow. She was horrified when they began eating it. Only later did she find out that they had poured lemonade there. "When you and Dan ate yellow snow."

Josh chortled. "We got you riled up. You started to tell my mom."

"I felt so dumb. You guys laughed at me, and it hurt my feelings."

"See!" Josh held his hands out from his sides, palms up. "It happens."

As they walked back to the cabin together, Bird pulled out a silver dollar and handed it to Josh. "Look what Aunt Trina gave me."

He eagerly studied both sides of it. She knew he'd like it because he collected coins. "It's a 1921 Liberty dollar," he exclaimed. "Mint condition."

"My aunt said it brought her luck."

"Like what?"

"One time a tornado skipped right over her house. Another time she took it to Las Vegas and won $500 playing blackjack."

Josh laughed. "Your aunt gambles?" Bird nodded as she took the coin back and buried it in her deepest pocket.

In the early evening, Josh and Bird set up lawn chairs down at the beach and covered the three picnic tables with bedsheets that passed for tablecloths. Then they reported back to the kitchen. "I had no idea it was so late," Mrs. Charkey said as she pulled two lemon poppy-seed cakes out of the oven. "I still have to shower." She handed Bird a plate of shrimp and Josh a platter of fruit kabobs and pointed toward the porch.

"I'm giving you two a mission," she told them when they returned. "Go down to the dock. Stall anyone who comes early." As she ducked into the bedroom they heard her yell, "Henry, if you don't get out of the shower, I'm coming in with you."

Down on the beach, Bird spotted Bill and Elliot speeding across the lake, their small boat planing on the rippling waves. "Are we the first ones here?" Bill asked as they climbed out onto the sand. Bird nodded.

"My mom's still in the shower," Josh announced. "We're supposed to stall you."

"Josh!" Bird elbowed him.

Elliot smiled and put a hand on each of their shoulders. "Let's give your mom time to dress." He guided them out to the end of the dock. Bill, Josh, and Bird settled on the bench. Elliot pulled off his sneakers and dangled his legs in the water.

"Too bad we haven't got a deck of cards," Bill said. "We could sneak in a game of hearts."

Josh jumped up. "I'll get some."

"No, no." Elliot shook his head. "Everyone will be here soon."

As they sat, the faint echo of voices drifted over from the far shore. "I hear there's news at your house, Bird," Bill said. She kicked at a nail poking up from a board. Why did he have to bring that up?

"Her mom's having a baby," Josh said. "On New Year's Day."

"What a way to start the year," Bird grumbled.

Elliot looked at her with quizzical eyes. "You're not happy?" Bird shrugged.

"You're like me when I was your age," Bill said. "I never wanted brothers or sisters." He leaned back against the bench and gazed out over the lake. "But there came a time when there was nothing I wanted more."

"Why?" Bird asked.

"Well, after my parents died, I didn't have a family anymore."

Elliot pulled his feet out of the water and twisted around to look at Bill. "What am I? Chopped liver?"

Bill smiled down at him. "Until I met Elliot, that is."

Bird wasn't persuaded. She couldn't think that far ahead when she had worries right now. Her mother wasn't acting herself lately. Yesterday, Bird peeked in her briefcase. Instead of work, it was full of mail-order catalogs for high chairs, car seats, baby clothes, and toys. All her mother thought about was the new baby! What about Bird? Did anyone think about her anymore?

Just then, a pontoon chugged around the bend into view, filled with party-goers. Josh and Bird led everyone up the hill to a small clearing among the pine trees still lit by the late-day sun. Mrs. Charkey waved and called to them all. As she welcomed each guest, she showed them her toenails painted red, white, and blue.

Bird and Josh listened to the adult chatter for a while, and then Josh signaled for her to follow him into the woods. When safely away, he started to whoop.

"Did you see my brother? With *that girl?*"

"Yeah," Bird replied. "He kissed her when they said hello. On the lips."

"*Eeuuw!* Don't even talk about it." The disgusted look on Josh's face made Bird giggle. She had been fascinated by the kiss, wondering what it felt like. But there was no discussing it with Josh. He pulled a package of Black Cat firecrackers out of his pocket.

"Where did you get those?"

"Joe." Bird inspected the black tissue-paper package with its bright-orange label. "After dark, I'm going to set some off," he whispered.

The smell of burgers sizzling on the grill wafted over to them as they followed the path back to the clearing. When they emerged, Joe waved for them to come over. He was standing with his arm around Ginny Gage. She had on a glistening gold jumpsuit and pumps with spike heels.

"Your little brother and his friend are so cute," Ginny said. "I think they're in puppy love."

"Nah," Joe scoffed. "They've been friends practically since they were born."

"I know the signs when I see them," Ginny insisted. Bird could feel her face reddening. Josh looked as if he had just swigged sour milk. Joe quickly swung Ginny around, pointing her toward the food. With each step she took toward the buffet, her spike heels poked holes into the grass.

"I think we have to play a little trick tonight," Josh said after they were gone. He whispered a plan to Bird.

When dinner was over, people drifted down to the beach. Josh and Bird watched Scotty set up his collection of Chinese fireworks. "When are you gonna start?" Josh asked.

Scotty looked up at the sky. "When it's good and dark. Another half hour."

Josh gave Bird a fiendish smile and then found his father. "Can we go swimming if Joe watches us?" Joe had his arm around Ginny as they sat on the bench at the end of the dock.

"It's been a long day. You feeling tired at all?" Mr. Charkey asked.

Josh shook his head vigorously. "Nope."

"Have you taken your AZT?" Josh nodded. "All right." Mr. Charkey called out to Joe, "Keep an eye on them while they swim."

Bird and Josh changed into their suits and were out at the trampoline in a flash. "It's now or never," Josh said to Bird, and they both started to swim in. Josh went all the way to shore, but Bird stopped at the end of the dock.

"Want to see me do water ballet?" she called. Bird plugged her nose and flipped back. She kicked her right leg into the air and slowly let it sink out of sight. Joe and Ginny applauded.

Meanwhile, Josh was creeping up behind them through the water. His arm was raised high in the air. "Now watch this," Bird called. She thrust both legs into the air and sank. More applause. Josh was plowing back through the water now, racing away.

BOOOOOOOMMM!!! A Black Cat firecracker exploded underneath the bench. Ginny lurched to her feet. She rocketed off the end of the dock in her gold jumpsuit. It was a long, powerful dive, like she had been shot from a cannon. Joe started to laugh. Then he saw Ginny's seething face appear above the water. "Go get them!" she cried, pointing to Josh and Bird escaping to the water trampoline.

Joe looked all around him. "Geronimo!" he shouted as he held his nose and jumped, shoes first, into the drink. He swam freestyle to the trampoline.

Ginny tossed her waterlogged high heels on the

dock and sidestroked out toward them. "You little monsters!" she said as she came up the ladder. She balanced herself on Joe's shoulder. "Oh, God, my makeup's running."

"Don't worry," Joe said as he pulled her shapely body close. "You look great."

"What's going on out there?" Mr. Charkey called from shore. "What was that explosion, Joe?"

"Just a firecracker, Dad."

"That's no example to set for Josh." Joe didn't say anything. But he gave Josh a look that said, unmistakably, you owe me big time.

They all went up to change. In the girls' cabin, Lisa gave Ginny a dry shirt and shorts. "Help yourself to a sweater in the closet if you want one," she said on her way out the door.

After Lisa left, Ginny glared at Bird. "This is a *designer* jumpsuit," she said, unzipping the wet garment. Bird shrugged. "Oh, it's just going to shrink up to nothing."

"Sorry," Bird told her. "But who knew you were going to dive in!"

When Bird returned to the beach, her mother and Mrs. Charkey were passing out slices of watermelon. She plopped down next to Josh and bit into a sweet, juicy piece.

The sky was the dark purple-blue color it turns just before black when Scotty shot off the first rocket. A burst of silver and blue rained down on the lake. Next came the red-pop green pop-pop of Roman candles. White whizzers flew up into the night, fizzling into the lake with a groan and a sigh. Bird watched Josh watch the sky, his bright eyes soaking in the dazzle of it all. She had an urge to grab on to him and hold him. If only this night, this week, this summer would never end.

Chapter 7

Puppy love. Puppy love! Bird was high in the Norway pine, thinking of Ginny's remark from the night before. I'm not in love with Josh. I couldn't be. Could I? What does love feel like, anyway? Does it tingle? Does it make your insides go to mush? Bird's friends Shawno and Jenny always had a secret crush on one boy or another. They spent hours plotting ways to have their secrets found out. What was it that made them act so crazed?

Bird played with lots of boys: softball, capture the flag, starlight-moonlight. She liked boys. But she had never had a crush. Of course, Josh was different. He knew practically everything about her. And she could tell him anything. Well, almost anything. She could never say she was in love with him. He'd unswallow his food.

Bird picked at some bark. She loosened a piece, which clicked down through the needles. Why did Ginny have to bring the whole thing up?

The next afternoon, as Bird stood on the end of the dock, Josh zoomed toward her in his fishing boat. She checked her insides. She didn't feel any tingling. That was a good sign.

"Look at this," Josh shouted as he beached the boat and walked over to her. He held up the front page of the *Nisswa Reporter* and pointed to the lead story:

RESORT OFFERS PRIZE FOR BIGGEST FISH

Ole Carlson, owner of Breezy Woods Resort, announced a fishing contest yesterday. First prize will be $300 and the winner's photo on the front page of this newspaper.

Last night, Irv LeBeck entered a four-pound walleyed pike. "With my sonic depth finder, I'll double that before the summer's over," said Mr. LeBeck.

"Can you imagine?" Josh asked, thrusting his arm into the air as if he were holding a huge fish. "Me! On the front page."

"What about Irv?"

Josh waved away the question. "That sonic thing doesn't work. We'll beat him."

They headed up the hill. "Looked at the nest lately?" Josh asked as they reached the poplar tree.

"No. Let's go up." Bird hoisted herself off the ground. She saw them when she was three branches into the tree. Eggs. "The nest is full!" she cried.

"I told you there'd be a lot," Josh said as he reached her branch. He counted nine eggs. "Isn't she smart? Look how she evened out the slant of the roof with pine needles."

"How long till the eggs hatch?" Bird asked.

"About a month, I think," Josh replied.

Later, when Bird's father returned from the golf course, he took them to Nisswa so they could buy lures at Bob's Bait and Tackle. Bird picked out the Red Eye devil, a silver disk with garnet-colored glass eyes that flashed and fooled the fish into biting. Josh chose a Rapala lure, a realistic model of the long minnows that northerns and walleyes loved to gobble. On the way out, Bird nudged Josh. "Look." Irv LeBeck's photograph stared down at them. He was laughing and holding his four pounder.

"Get me outta here," Josh said. They charged out the door. Josh raised a high five. "We gonna let Irv beat us?"

Bird slapped his hand. "No way!"

After supper, Josh and Bird got out their heavy action rods, fastened on the new lures, and rode out to their favorite spot. The sun was barely peeking over the pointed evergreens, about to disappear for the night. They trolled back and forth from the public landing to Breezy Woods. On their third pass, Josh's pole jumped. "Whoa!" he called. "Took it hard." He cut the motor and began quickly winding in.

Josh spun his reel, his pole pointed in the air. "He's fighting." Josh played the fish until it finally showed itself six feet from the boat. He brought in the last few yards of line, and Bird scooped the fish up with the net.

"That's a beaut!" she said as Josh held up the long blackish green northern.

"Say good-bye to first place, Irv," Josh said as he pull-started the small motor. At Breezy Woods, Ole Carlson came out on the end of the dock and hooked a scale in the mouth of the fish.

"Is Josh in first?" Bird cried.

"Wait, let me read this. Yes! Four pounds and four ounces."

"I knew it!" shouted Josh. "You want my picture now?"

Mr. Carlson laughed. "C'mon, we'll put you up in place of Irv."

A miserable patch of weather took hold toward the middle of July. Thunderstorms gave way to showers followed by drizzle and dampness. Josh and Bird played Monopoly at her cabin and read comics at his. Hearts and Oh Hell! with Bill and Elliot filled one afternoon. By then, Bird was gripped with cabin fever. She talked her father into taking them to Paul Bunyan Land in Brainerd one overcast day. They rode the Ferris wheel in the gloom. Josh and Bird longed to get back to the water. It seemed that blue sky would never return.

Then, as surely as they had rolled in, the clouds blew away. Diamonds shimmered on the lake as the sun reflected off its rippling surface. Out at the diving platform, amid the sparkle, Bird floated on her stomach, holding her breath, head and arms hanging down into the water. Ever since lunch, her back had ached and this position in the water eased it.

She pulled up for a breath and heard Josh call to her from the trampoline. "Look," he shouted, pointing. Joe was running toward the lake with Ginny struggling in his arms.

"Stop, Joe! Stop!" she yelled. Joe kicked up a great splash as he hit the water, lunged forward until he was chest deep, and plunged them both under. He backstroked to the trampoline with Ginny chasing him.

Josh and Bird returned to their underwater competition. Neither had yet done ten lengths. While Josh was under, Bird spied on Joe and Ginny sitting above her on the platform. She heard them murmuring, but couldn't make out the words. Then Ginny reached over and kissed Joe on the lips.

Josh's head popped out of the water. Bird hushed him and pointed at the kissing couple. Josh's nose wrinkled, and he gulped a mouthful of lake water. He aimed at their entwined faces and let loose, splattering their foreheads and cheeks.

"Hey!" Joe shouted as he and Ginny pulled apart.

"What is it?" Ginny cried, looking into the sky. Josh loaded another mouthful and let it rip right at her. "Cut that out," she barked at him, at last finding the source of the spray. But Josh was waging a full-scale attack. He reloaded and fired.

"Enough!" Joe yelled, standing up. He leaped off the platform. Josh swam like a shark toward shore, but his brother overtook him near the end of the dock. He grabbed Josh by his bathing suit and hiked him out of the water as the suit stretched halfway up his chest.

"Let me go. Let me go," Josh pleaded. "I'll never do it again."

"Promise?"

"I swear. I swear." Joe let him down.

"Unless you kiss Ginny again," Josh yelled as soon as he was free. He hooted and raced for the diving platform. But Joe didn't chase him. He waved to Ginny to come in, and the two of them dried off and went up the hill.

Back at the diving platform, Josh edged out onto the trampoline and lay down. Bird hoisted herself up onto the planking, and the two of them basked in the sun. The afternoon drifted lazily by.

"I'm going for ten," Josh said, standing. "Will you count?"

"Okay." Bird sat up. There was a wetness in the crotch of her suit. That's funny. The rest of her suit was dry. She reached down and put her hand there. It was warm and wet. She looked. *Blood!* Seeping out of her yellow suit. *Her period!*

Bird slid into the water in a split second. She dove under and raced for shore. She had to get away from Josh. Bird made it inside the L-shaped dock on one breath. But what was she going to do now? Her pads were at home in the dresser. "Hey," Josh called after her. "Where are you going?"

Bird tore out of the water, grabbed her towel, and wrapped it around her waist. "To the bathroom," she yelled back as she ripped up the hill toward the yellow cabin.

Please, please, please don't let me see anyone. She took a shortcut off the path. Pinecones gouged into the arches of her feet as she ran. How was she going to get home?

Bird yanked open the screen door of the girls' cabin and froze. Lisa was lying on the bed reading. Bird whisked past her into the bathroom and slammed the door. She pulled off the towel and inspected the stain on her suit.

"Bird, are you okay?" Lisa's voice jolted her. Bird was silent, pretending she wasn't there. She realized that it wouldn't work and opened the door a crack.

"I just got my period," she said, her cheeks flushing. "My first one."

"Oh, Birdie!"

"I don't have my pads." She opened the door a little further.

Lisa touched her on the shoulder. "Don't worry, we'll find something." She walked to the closet.

"Let's see, I've got tampons." Tampons! Bird had no idea how to use one. And she was not about to. "Mother must have some pads," Lisa said. "Be right back." She pushed open the screen door and disappeared.

Bird's heart fluttered while she pulled off her bathing suit and wrapped herself in a towel. Imagine. She could have a child now. She hadn't even kissed a boy yet!

Lisa came back into the cabin moments later. "Here we go." She handed over a blue box, and Bird hurried into the bathroom with her shorts and shirt. She came out dressed, smiling sheepishly. "Come here," Lisa said gently. "I'll brush your hair." Bird's embarrassment drained away as she gave herself over to Lisa's hands. The older girl stood over Bird, stroking her long, wet hair. "It's kind of a shocker, isn't it? Just happens all of a sudden." The soothing pressure of the firm bristles massaged Bird's scalp. "I was at the movies when mine first came."

"What did you do?" Bird liked the way they were talking—confidentially.

"Dragged my girlfriend down to the bathroom

and made a pad out of rolled-up toilet paper. My friend was jealous because she hadn't gotten hers yet." Bird pressed her head back against the brush. "Are you glad to have yours, Bird?"

"Well, now I can't go swimming."

"Sure you can. Just put on a pad right away when you get out of the water." That sounded like a hassle to Bird and she frowned. "Don't worry, you'll wear tampons before long. You can go in the water with them."

Lisa tossed the brush onto the dresser and plopped on the bed next to Bird. "Don't you feel lots older?" Bird nodded solemnly. Lisa gave her a squeeze. "You're practically grown-up now."

Filled with the significance of what had just happened, Bird walked slowly toward the beach. Josh sat on the end of the dock, his feet dangling in the water. "You're dressed! How come?"

Bird blushed. Should she tell him? Why not? He really should know. "You're with a woman now."

"*What* are you talking about?"

Bird stood erect and cast a serious glance at him. "I just got my period."

"You did? That's why you took off without me?"

Josh shrugged. "I know all about that. I bought tampons for Lisa once at the Peoria Store. Slender regular." Bird wished all boys could be like Josh. He was so easy to talk to. "Can't you swim?"

"I'm not going in anymore today."

"You were supposed to count laps for me."

"I still will." Bird raced off the dock, grabbed her canoe and shoved it into the water. "Beat you out there." Josh was hanging off the diving platform with both arms when she arrived. Bird looked down as he hyperventilated. "Go, Josh! Let's see you do ten."

"I have news." Bird's mother was practically singing when she arrived at the cabin the next weekend. But she wouldn't say a word until she took off her dress and had a cranberry spritzer in her hand. They settled on the deck in front of the cabin. "It's about the baby," she said, patting her stomach. Of course, thought Bird. The baby. What else? "I had a sonogram today. It showed whether it's a girl or a boy."

"Which is it, dear?" her father asked. "You're keeping us in suspense."

"A girl," she announced with a sigh.

Bird's father jumped up and kissed his wife. "Another girl," he cooed, and then he kissed Bird, too.

Bird didn't say anything. A girl. A boy would have been better.

"I've been thinking of names," her mother said. "How do you like Virginia?"

"Virginia! Mother, you can't keep naming us after states."

"Well, do you have an idea? Something as beautiful as Carolina?" She beamed at her daughter.

"What about Amanda?" Her first doll.

"Hmm. That's nice," her mother said, glancing at her husband. Bird saw a look pass between them.

"Yes. It has a ring to it," her father agreed. And though they discussed many others, they kept coming back to that one.

"I love the name Amanda," her mother said that night as she turned out the light in Bird's room. A tickle of excitement ran through Bird at the thought of having a sister. Her mother sat down on the edge of the bed, reached under Bird's pajama top, and began to rub her back. Bird wanted to protest, but the touch was warm and smooth against her skin. It felt so good, she let it go on.

As Bird started to drift off to sleep, she remembered something. "Mom?"

"Yes?"

"It happened this week. I got my period."

"You did? Where?"

"At Melody Shores."

"Were you okay?"

"Uh-huh. Lisa was there, and she helped me."

"Oh, Carolina." Mrs. Birdsong put her head down on her daughter's back and hugged her. "You're growing up so fast."

The next day, after an afternoon of swimming, Bird changed into dry clothes in the girls' cabin. She spied two comic books lying on the floor below Lisa's pillow. She picked up *Teen Romance*. On the cover a beautiful girl was sobbing: "My best friend stole the only man I'll ever love." She picked up the other one, called *Love Comics*. Bird began flipping through it until she came to a page entitled "The Love Quiz." Underneath the title it said, "Five questions will tell you if you really love him." Bird jerked the comic book wide open and peered down at the questions.

"1. Does your heart race when you think about him?" She pictured Josh and put her hand to her chest. Her heart was pounding. She gulped and went on to the next question.

"2. Does time seem to fly by when you're with him?" Lord! Bird remembered days when she had arrived at Melody Shores after lunch, and it seemed Josh's mother was calling them for dinner only moments later. Surely, she would answer no to all the rest. She read on.

"3. Do you dream about him at night?" I can't believe this! Bird thought. Just the night before she had dreamed of them swimming laps. She slapped the comic book closed. This was stupid. You couldn't tell anything from a quiz like this. Bird got up and rushed to the door. She put her hand on the knob and then stopped, went back, and grabbed the comic again. She rifled through the pages until she found the quiz and read the next question.

"4. When he goes away, do you count the days until he returns?" Oh no! When Josh had gone to

Iowa last summer, Bird checked the calendar every day to see when he was due back. She felt dizzy. She didn't want to go on, but she had to. There must be one question to which she could answer no. And if the answer to any question was no, she reasoned, then you were not in love. She read the last question.

"5. If you had to choose between fishing with him and shopping for clothes with your girlfriend, would you go fishing?" Bird gasped and threw herself facedown on the bed. The answer to every question was yes. Ginny was right. It *was* love!

Chapter 8

If Josh noticed that Bird was acting strangely the next few days, he didn't say anything. Perhaps he thought she had become fascinated with the field grass and the treetops, for she dared not look into his eyes. He would see her lovesick condition. Night after night, Bird refused to go fishing. She had no idea what she might do alone with him out on the water. It was enough to give her a panic attack.

"What's the matter?" Josh finally asked one evening. "You're acting funny."

"I am?" She sat on the beach, running her fingers through the sand, trying to think of some explanation.

"Yes! How come you won't go fishing? Are you mad at me?"

Oh, how she wished that were it. She kept her eyes fixed on the lake. "No, I'm not mad."

"What, then? Is it because you're a woman now? You gonna start putting on makeup, like Ginny?" Josh waltzed across the beach in front of her, wiggling his hips. "You like my *designer* jumpsuit?" he asked in a high-pitched voice, pointing at his old camp shorts. Bird couldn't help giggling. "I heard that." Josh rushed over to her. "You laughed." He knelt and brought his face near hers, his eyes pleading with her.

She'd never noticed before how long and dark his eyelashes were. Bird snapped her lids closed. She had to shift her thoughts or else be discovered. Peas and carrots. Bird forced herself to think of vegetables as she looked back at him. Peas and carrots. Peas and carrots.

"Aren't we still buddies?" he asked, searching her face.

Asparagus. Rutabaga. "Course we are."

"Okay, then." Josh stood and headed for his boat. "Let's go fishing." Bird let out a long breath. It worked. He hadn't noticed anything in her eyes. She rose and walked slowly toward the boat.

Josh ran them to the far side of Ossaway Island, and they dropped anchor. Before long, another boat sped around the bend. Bird recognized the whiskery, potbellied man who bore down on them. Irv LeBeck.

"Hey, you're in my spot," he yelled.

Josh glanced at him and then cast out a long, flowing line. "Guess you can't reserve a spot."

"Well, don't you follow me around anymore." Irv tossed his anchor over the bow. He fished twenty feet from them all night, without a strike, while Josh and Bird each pulled in a good-sized walleye. When Josh landed a small northern, Irv started up his motor and steered himself close enough to grab the side of their boat. "What the hell kind of lures are you using?"

Josh kicked his tackle box closed. "Just hooks," he said. "We don't bother with worms any-more."

Irv grunted. "How old are you? Little wiseass!"

"Twenty-four," Josh answered. "I'm a midget."

"Yeah! Grow up, then." Irv spit into the lake and revved his motor. "See ya, shrimp," he snarled, roaring off.

The next night, as they fished in the same spot, Irv's boat planed across the lake toward them. He cut the motor to trolling speed, stood, and held up an enormous northern. "Eight and a half pounds," he called out, giving his pelvis a little victory shake. Bird hoped he would fall into the lake. But instead, Irv sat down and sped off toward Breezy Woods, his laughter ringing off the water.

"There goes first place," Josh moaned. "How will we ever beat that?"

"I don't know." Bird shook her head. "That fish was huge."

The next night Bird heard a car door slam shut. She glimpsed her father coming up from the Charkeys' driveway. He had on his moth-eaten, old college sweater, which was beyond hope of patching. For years, each time he took it off Bird's mother suggested it go in the garbage. "Not a thing wrong with it," her father would insist as he carefully slipped it over a nail in the broom closet.

Josh's father appeared out of the cabin in an equally tattered cardigan. "You dressed up," he said to Mr. Birdsong. They both laughed as if it weren't the millionth time they had seen each other in those sweaters.

"Josh," his father called to him. "Did you take your AZT this afternoon?"

"Shoot." Josh pinched himself on the arm. "I forgot."

"Well, don't forget again," his father scolded as Josh and Bird headed off to his cabin.

Bird watched as Josh popped the pill into his mouth and put his lips under the tap. He leaned his head back and swallowed. "What a drag—taking these all the time."

They went back outside and wandered around, finally settling in the grass next to Mill Pond. The night was silent except for a lone cricket chirping. "Is your dad mad at you?" Bird asked.

"Nah, not really." Josh scowled and pulled his knees up under his chest.

"What's the matter, then?"

Josh shook his head. "Dan's not going to Madison Junior High with me in the fall." Dan had been Josh's best friend all through grade school.

"Why not?"

"They're moving to California." Josh drilled his chin down on his knee. "He's my only good friend who was going there."

"You'll make new friends."

Josh shook his head. "Not when they find out I'm HIV-positive." He threw himself back on the ground. "You know what they'll say then?" He clapped his hand over his eyes. "That I'm gay."

"Gay? Why would they say that?"

"Oh, I don't know. A lot of gay people have AIDS."

"Can't you tell them—"

Josh sat up abruptly. "I don't want to tell them anything. I don't want them talking about me." He pushed his hair back from his forehead once and then again. "Why can't Dan stay here!"

Bird was silent, her mind racing. What was so bad about being gay? Bill and Elliot were. Well, some kids probably would be mean about it. Especially boys. With everything else, Josh shouldn't have to worry about finding friends. What if *she* went to Madison? It was a magnet school. Her father had even asked if she wanted to go there. "Josh, I could go to Madison with you."

The second the words were out of her mouth, she wanted to take them back. Had she no shame? She was chasing him, pure and simple. He was going to see that.

Josh's face lit up. "You mean it? Would you really?"

The meaning of what she was offering suddenly hit her. She would have to ride a bus clear across town every day. Winter mornings would be dark. Shawno and Jenny were going to Longfellow, her neighborhood school. But he needed her! And she couldn't go back on her offer now. "I do, Josh. I mean it."

Bird mentioned her plan the next night as her father made a salad. "You said I could go to Madison in the fall, right?"

He looked up at her from the yellow bell pepper he was cutting. "Yes. It's a very good school."

"And it would be okay with Mom, too?"

"Uh-huh. But I thought you had decided on Longfellow. Isn't that where your friends are going?" He scraped the pepper slices into a wooden bowl filled with romaine and tomatoes.

"Not all my friends."

Just then, a car pulled into the driveway. Bird's mother had arrived from the city. "Quick. Put these in the fridge." Bird's father handed her a bowl of sliced strawberries. Then he hid a plate of shortcake in the cupboard. "I made her favorite dessert again."

After dinner, all of them stuffed with strawberry shortcake, they settled in the living room. Bird curled up on the sofa with a book, and her mother slid next to her. "What are you reading?" she asked. Bird showed her the cover: *Bridge to Terabithia* by Katherine Paterson. "Can we read together?" her mother asked.

Bird nodded and described what had already happened in the story. Then they took turns reading to each other. When they got to a sad part, Mrs. Birdsong's voice grew thick. She cleared her throat, read on haltingly, and then stopped.

Bird looked up at her. Was she crying? Bird took the book from her mother's hands. "We can't stop now. I have to know how it ends."

On Saturday night, Joe took Bird, Josh, and Ginny to the movies in Nisswa. They bought tickets under the old-fashioned marquee and headed up to the last row of seats in the balcony. Before the previews were over, Joe had his arm around Ginny. Bird tried not to notice. Josh was sitting right next to her. She jammed her hands in her jeans pockets and concentrated on brussels sprouts.

In the movie, an American reporter fell in love with a French woman in Paris during World War II. In the midst of an air raid, the lovers were separated. The reporter had a square jaw, intense green eyes, and strong arms covered with golden hair. Bird couldn't take her eyes off those arms. His voice was so low and soothing. She put her hand on her chest. Her insides were tingling!

The reporter was at last reunited with his love after V-E Day. Bird imagined herself as the French woman, falling into the reporter's arms as he kissed her forehead, cheeks, and lips. She trembled, wanting so much to know how it felt. The lights came up and Bird sighed.

"Pretty good," Josh said to her. "Until the lip-sucking part at the end."

She stared at him and, for the first time, imagined being held by him as the reporter had held the French woman. The thought made her step backward, and she shook it out of her head.

As they left, Bird puzzled over the last question in "The Love Quiz": Would you choose fishing with him or shopping? She'd rather go fishing with anyone—even Irv LeBeck—than go shopping for clothes. Could the quiz have been wrong?

On the way home from Nisswa, Bird sat inches from Josh in the back of Joe's truck. Though the night air was warm and the sky was bright with a million stars, she didn't have to conjure up images of stewed tomatoes. Her thoughts were far away, in Paris, where she was wrapped in the arms of a man with green eyes.

Chapter 9

The first of August arrived with a jolt. At the end of the month, Bird's family would take in the dock, drain the pipes, and close up the cabin for the year. Her mind kept returning to this, like her tongue finding the hole left by a pulled tooth.

It must have bothered Josh, too, because he was quiet all that day. In the evening, they played double solitaire in his cabin. At one point, he started coughing. Bird wondered if he was getting a cold. "I better go," she said, after they had finished another game. The daylight was fading into dusk. She had to have the canoe home before dark.

As they walked past the front door of the main cabin, Josh started to cough again. He clapped his hand over his mouth and stifled it, hurrying away from the cabin. When they were halfway down the hill to the beach, he let the cough out. Bird looked at him quizzically.

"You know how my mom is," he explained. "She'll drag me to the doctor just for a cold." Bird knew Josh hated to go to the doctor, but she worried about him keeping things from his parents.

The next afternoon, Bird found Josh at Melody Shores lying back in a beach chair. He had on his swimming trunks, and a beach towel was draped over his shoulders. "Been in yet?" she asked.

"Uh-uh," he answered, pulling the towel more tightly around himself. There were goose bumps on his bare chest.

Bird plopped down in the chair next to him. "My dad wants to have a wiener roast on Saturday. Your whole family is invited." Josh looked at her blankly. "You want to come?" she asked.

"Okay," he answered in a flat voice, as if she had

offered him the chance to help clean her room. He started coughing.

"How's your cold?" she asked.

"Okay." They sat quietly for a few minutes, and Bird wondered if he was all right. "I'm boiling hot," Josh said suddenly, jerking the towel off his body. "Let's go in."

They made their way slowly out to the trampoline. Once there, Bird inhaled, exhaled, inhaled again, and dived under. She managed eight lengths. Not her best, but she usually could do more on the second or third try. Then Josh plunged under. She could see him through the water, swimming along the cross-boards. One. Two. He rushed to the surface. Josh gasped for air, hanging from the diving platform with one arm.

"What's wrong?"

"Ran out . . ."—he sucked in—"of . . . breath." Josh started for shore, dog-paddling, but hadn't gone five feet when his head dipped under. Bird lunged for him and raised his upper body. He came up coughing and clutched her shoulder as she struggled with him to shore.

She threw a towel around him and raced up the hill. Bird burst into the main cabin, shouting, "It's Josh! Hurry!"

When Josh's mother saw him huddled on the beach, shivering, she broke into a run. She felt his forehead. "Oh, honey, you're burning up." She looked up the hill. "Can you walk?" Josh tried to rise and collapsed back onto the sand, coughing violently. "We're going to the hospital," she told him.

"*No!*" he wailed. "I'm okay."

Supporting him on either side, they walked toward the car. "I can't . . . get my breath," he gasped at the top of the hill. They practically carried him the last few yards and tried to lay him in the backseat, but he wanted to sit up. It was easier to breathe. Mrs. Charkey spoke quickly to Lisa, and then she and Bird jumped in front and roared off. On the dirt road around the lake, an old man puttering along in his sedan blocked their progress. Mrs. Charkey laid on her horn and raced past him, spewing clouds of dust into the air.

"Mom!" Josh called out as they sped along. "What's wrong with me?"

She craned her head around as she drove. "We'll find out. Just stay still." She raced through a red light and turned left onto the highway, gripping the wheel like she was driving a tank.

Josh's breath came in shallow, quick gulps, and he looked blue around the lips. Every time he coughed, Bird's muscles tensed up. The half-hour drive to Brainerd seemed endless. Finally, Mrs. Charkey swerved into the emergency room entrance of Crow Wing County Hospital. They helped Josh into the waiting room. He and his mother disappeared down a long, lime green hallway.

Bird was suddenly alone. She sat down in an orange plastic chair near an old woman who was slumped forward, wheezing. The chair pressed into Bird's tailbone. She moved to a different one and then a third. She waited and waited. When would they come back out?

When she couldn't sit still any longer, she got up and went to the window. She thought about what she had learned from the AIDS pamphlet her father had given her. HIV was building up in Josh's body, eating away at the white blood cells of his immune system. One day—she had no idea how soon—he would get pneumonia or some other infection. His body wouldn't be able to fight it off. Bird pressed her head hard against the window. Outside, the wilted shrubbery lining the sidewalk had turned yellow.

A station wagon screeched to a halt in front of her. Out jumped a man and a hysterical girl. Bird didn't want to look, but she couldn't help herself. Stuck in the girl's swollen, bloody eye was a fishhook. The cut fishing line trailed down her face. They came inside. "I didn't see her," Bird heard the man explaining. "She came up behind when I was casting." The girl was sobbing now, and she and the man disappeared down the sickening green hallway. Would she trade places with that girl if it would make Josh better? Would she give up one eye?

Bird went back to her chair and started to count backward from one thousand to pass the time. She was almost finished when Joe strode into the emergency room. She ran to him.

"Bird! What happened? What's wrong with Josh?"

She told him all that she knew. And then they waited. Joe kept going up to the nurse's station only to be told they were still running tests.

Finally, Mrs. Charkey came out to them. She looked shaken. Joe reached for her and put his arm around her shoulders. "They're admitting him."

"What for?" Joe asked.

"They think it's pneumonia."

"Oh, Mom."

"I have to call your father in the city." She opened her coin purse and fumbled for quarters. "Josh is going to Room 801. Go stay with him while I talk to Dad."

Joe and Bird took the elevator to the eighth floor. Josh was in the hallway on a gurney, hooked to an intravenous bag hanging from a pole. Plastic prongs jabbed into his nose feeding him oxygen from a portable tank. He waved limply, the hospital bracelet slipping up his arm.

An orderly wheeled Josh into the double room and transferred his weak body onto the hospital bed. His gown slipped up, and Bird looked away from his pale skin. Nurses came in and out, checking the I.V. bag, taking his temperature and pulse, adjusting the automatic bed into a partly upright position. Mrs. Charkey joined them shortly and sat on her son's bed. "Dad's on his way."

Soon a young pediatrician arrived. She took the chart hanging on the end of Josh's bed and quickly scanned it. The doctor pulled down the lower lid of one of Josh's eyes and then the other. She put a stethoscope in her ears and listened to his chest. "Take a deep breath," she instructed. She yanked the instrument down to her neck. "Is it a productive cough?" she asked Josh's mother. "Does he bring anything up?"

"I don't know. Do you, Josh?" He shrugged.

Bird tried to read the doctor's face. Calm. Intense. But no clue was there. Mrs. Charkey and the doctor stepped out into the hallway and Joe followed.

Alone, Bird moved next to Josh on his bed.

Sadness surged inside her, rising from her chest into her throat. She swallowed it back so it wouldn't get to her eyes. "You scared?" His eyes welled up and he pushed himself over onto his side, away from her. He hit his pillow once and then again. Bird bit her lip to keep from making any sound. She could hear him struggling.

Josh's mother came back into the room followed by Joe, who looked more serious than Bird had ever seen him. Mrs. Charkey sat on Josh's bed and took his hand.

"What is it?" Josh asked.

She started to answer, her voice cracked, and she turned away. "Tell him, Joe."

"Guess you have pneumonia, buddy."

"Oh, geez." Josh put his hand over his chest and sank back into the pillow. He started coughing again. Mrs. Charkey turned back to him and stroked his forehead. "What will they do for it?" Josh asked.

"Give you antibiotics," his mother answered. "It'll clear up."

"How long will it take?"

She shook her head. "You'll be here a few days, at least."

"I'm stuck in the hospital? And you're all going back to Whitefish?"

"I'm not," his mother answered. "I'll stay here with you."

It was dusk as Bird rode home with Joe in his truck. She was sure the doctor had said more than what they told Josh. "What's wrong with him?"

"Pneumonia. But they're not sure what kind."

"There are different kinds?"

"Yeah. There's regular pneumonia. Anyone could get that. And there's PCP."

"What's that?"

"A much worse kind of pneumonia." Joe's voice choked. "Only people with AIDS get PCP."

AIDS. The word bounced around the cab of the truck like an angry hornet trapped inside. If Josh had it, how much time was left? "When will they know?" Bird cried.

"In a couple of days. They have to do a procedure. Take a tissue sample from his lungs and send it to the lab."

There were fishing boats on Upper Rhoda Pond as they drove past. How could anyone fish! Bird wanted to roll down the window and scream at them.

At home, she told her father what had happened, and they called her mother in the city. But nothing her parents said made her feel any better. At dinner, she ferociously devoured two hamburgers. When she finished, it felt as if she had swallowed a rat that was gnawing at her stomach. She couldn't sit still, so she went down to the dock.

The world seemed unreal. She and Josh should have been bringing in their catch about now. Instead, he was lying in a white gown with an I.V. needle in his arm. Darkness seeped out of the sky and surrounded her. Out on the lake, she heard the quavering laughter of a loon. *Ha-oo-oo. Ha-oo-oo.* Bird usually loved the eerie sound. But tonight it gave her a chill. She hurried off the dock. The loon hooted at her again. "Shut up," she shouted as she picked up a rock and hurled it at the noisy fowl.

As she tried to sleep that night, Bird counted each time the mantle chimes rang. Every quarter hour. Over and over the five notes played, like dreary church bells. Bird drifted off to sleep. She was inside a church: St. Paul's Cathedral, massive and hulking. She passed through a carved-stone archway and climbed the heavy steps. She was in a hospital ward, but no one was there. She looked in every room. The beds were empty, the sheets strewn. Then she saw Mrs. Charkey sitting, staring. Josh lay next to her. Tubes were shoved up his nose and down his throat. His I.V. was hooked somewhere beneath his gown. The sallow skin on his face hung from his cheekbones.

She moved toward him. A nun in her white habit stepped in Bird's way. "Let him rest," she commanded.

"I have to see him."

"No."

Josh saw Bird. His thin hand stirred. He lifted it to his heart and tapped slowly. Once. Twice. Three times. She must go to him! Take his hand. The nun ushered her away. "No! No! No!" Bird cried.

Hearing her own voice, she woke up, tangled in the damp sheets. The alarm clock blinked 3:30. She wanted to rush down to the dock, rage into the depths of Whitefish Lake, and swim until she disappeared. She could not bear to watch Josh die.

Chapter 10

Light finally crept around the edges of the window shade in Bird's tiny room. She rose wearily and doused her face with cold water. Out in the kitchen, the brightness of the day hurt her eyes. She poured herself a glass of milk to settle her rumbling stomach. *Brrringgg! Brrringgg!* The phone startled her, and she spilled milk on her nightgown. No one called this early. It had to be about Josh. "Hello."

"Bird. You up?"

"Oh. Hi, Joe." She wondered if he had had trouble sleeping, too.

"Wanna go fishing?" he asked.

"Aren't you going to the hospital?"

"Can't go this early." There was a pause. "Gotta do something to pass the time."

"Okay," she said. "Maybe we'll catch a northern bigger than Irv's."

"Josh would love it," he replied. She heard a catch in his voice.

Joe took her to the south side of Whitefish Lake near the mouth of the Pine River. "This is where walleyes have breakfast," he said as they trolled along about twenty feet from shore. The sun was warm on Bird's back. Would Josh ever get to do this again?

Joe made a U-turn and cut the motor. "Reel in slowly," he whispered. The morning grew still. A fish jumped, rippling the shallow waters near shore. Joe nodded at her as both of them teased their lures through the weedy-green bottom.

The silence was broken by Bird's shout. "I've got one." The fish was a fighter. Her biceps tightened as she worked the line. Could this be the one? Joe had the net ready and flipped the walleye into the boat. A decent size, but not a trophy.

That morning, they caught five between them. Though their stringer full of fish was impressive, there was no need to weigh in at Breezy Woods when they were done. As Joe used an oar to propel them out of the weeds, an idea struck Bird. "Let's take the fish to Josh."

"To the hospital?"

"Why not?" Until now, Bird had felt helpless. But there was one thing she could do: take Josh a piece of the world outside. Back at Melody Shores, Joe took the stringer of fish off the side of the boat, put it in a metal bucket full of lake water, and set it in the back of the truck. "We can't just walk in with a pail of walleyes," Bird told him.

Joe motioned her to follow. From the cluttered closet in his parents' bedroom, he pulled out a vinyl bowling bag and removed the blue-swirled ball. "Last Thanksgiving, my mother carried a turkey in this to my sister's."

"Really?"

"Yup. She didn't think you could buy a good bird in New York City." Joe turned the bag upside down and shook it out. "I guess it'll work for fish, too."

They loaded it next to the bucket and set off for Brainerd. Through the back window of the cab, Bird kept an eye on the sloshing pail. They parked two blocks away from the hospital on a street of old, wood-frame houses that were painted white, cornflower blue, and mint green. Glancing nervously over his shoulder, Joe transferred the walleyes into the bowling bag.

"Let's run," Bird urged as she zipped the bag shut. They sprinted off. Joe slowed her as they reached the hospital sidewalk. Erect, eyes staring straight ahead, they stepped to the entrance. A doctor reached the door at the same time they did and opened it for them. "Been bowling?" he inquired.

Bird was about to bolt for the truck when Joe replied, "Had a good day. Got five strikes." Bird stifled a whoop as they hightailed it for the elevators. The doors opened on the eighth floor, and the smell of ointments and disinfectant rushed in.

They barreled past the nurses' station. "Excuse me!" Bird turned and looked. A nurse with red hair was staring straight at them. Joe was going to have to do the talking. She couldn't lie to save her life.

Out of the corner of her eye, she saw the bowling bag move as one of the walleyes flipped its tail.

The nurse leaned over the counter. Her name tag bobbed at them: Lou Ann Lodish, R.N. "Where's the fire?" she asked.

"Sorry, Nurse," Joe said in his most polite voice. "We're visiting my little brother."

She pointed down at the bowling bag. "What's in there?"

Joe glanced at Bird, but she stared straight ahead. "What does it look like?" he answered. The nurse nodded at them, and they walked slower than old dogs to Room 801. Josh's mother was on his bed with him. Mr. Charkey and Lisa were rummaging through cookie tins.

Josh sat up when he saw them. His lips were not blue anymore. "Dad said you went fishing."

"All morning," Bird told him. "They were bitin' like mosquitoes." As she spoke, Joe lifted out the stringer heavy with fish.

Josh's eyes lit up. "You guys!" He inspected their catch. "How did you get them in *here*?"

"I'll tell you!" boomed a voice from the doorway. Nurse Lodish stood there, one arm on her hip.

"Snuck 'em in right under my nose." Joe flung the fish back into the bag. The nurse's face relaxed into a grin, and she walked into the room. "I've seen puppies, cats, even a hamster come in here." She gave Josh a paper cup with pills in it. "First time we've had fish." Joe lifted the stringer again. "Wish my boyfriend would catch some like that," said the nurse. "Haven't had fresh fish all summer."

"Want a couple of these?" Joe offered.

"Now you're talking. Drop a couple by on your way out." She scribbled on Josh's chart and headed for the door. "Say, I wonder if the surgeon will fillet them for me."

After lunch, Nurse Lodish returned to take Josh for another test. She announced that the pediatrician wanted to see Josh's parents in the morning. All of the test results would be back then. Bird stiffened. Was it regular pneumonia or PCP? She glanced at Josh. He was asleep! It was only two o'clock. She couldn't remember the last time he had taken a nap. Even when they were little and their mothers had put them down together, Josh would chatter on and on and they never slept a wink.

She bit down on a hangnail and ripped it off her thumb. The torn skin smarted. Josh must have been up in the night like she was. That was it. But an inner voice nagged. AIDS. It saps your strength. The rat started gnawing at her stomach again.

When Bird got home that afternoon, there was a note on the door saying that her father had gone up to Burkett Farm. She found the key under the flowerpot on the deck. As she fiddled with the lock, the sound of quacking floated to her. She crept down to the poplar and hoisted herself into the tree. Could it be? Yes. The eggs were hatching.

The mother duck was standing beside the nest as the last two shells cracked open. Nine ducklings, wet and gray, padded around the roof, dumb and lovable. They knocked one another down as they tried out their webbed feet for the first time. Their heads turned this way and that.

When they were all out of the nest, the mother duck fluttered down past the picture window and landed on the grass below. None of the ducklings followed. Mother waddled back and forth, quacking furiously. Finally, one duckling heeded her call and jumped. It fell to the ground and landed with a *plump!* The others followed in turn. All of them dropped safely down, except one. It went to the edge, looked over, and then hurried back to the nest. It would not budge no matter how much its mother scolded. Finally, the mother turned and led her brood away. Was she going to leave it there?

After a few steps, the wayward duckling leaped off and scampered into line, not about to be left behind. The ducks all made their way into the woods.

Bird climbed down from the tree and lay back in the field grass. The firmness of the earth pressed against her. She could hear bees in the clover gathering nectar to make honey for the next generation. A sulphur butterfly flitted around the grass seed heads looking for a place to lay her eggs. Under Bird's body, rotting birch leaves from last fall crumbled into the fertile soil. In the vast world, the force of life surged ahead. Bird sucked in a breath of the fragrant air and fell fast asleep.

Chapter 11

Josh's room was empty when Bird got there late the next morning. "He's having a shower, hon," Nurse Lodish told her. "Be back in fifteen." Bird dug her fingernails into the flesh of her palms as she headed for the hospital gift shop. Josh's parents were probably meeting with the doctor right now.

Just beyond the cooler filled with roses and gladiolus, Bird spied the face of her green-eyed movie star on a Hollywood magazine. Blazing across the cover were the words EXCLUSIVE SWIMSUIT PHOTOS. She looked around quickly and then grabbed it. She had to buy it. As she paid for the magazine and a Kit Kat bar, Bird's pulse raced. The clerk surely knew that she was thinking dirty thoughts.

"Bird," Josh called when she returned to his room. "What took you so long to get here?" His dark eyes bored into her. She dragged the guest chair over to his bed and sank into it. "I gotta ask you something," he said, lowering his voice. His hand trembled slightly.

"Okay."

"I was awake last night. Thinking."

"About what?"

He leaned toward her, his skin glistening in the light from the window. "What happens when you die?"

Bird flinched. "Josh, don't think like that."

"Why not? I know I might have AIDS." His eyes challenged her. "I knew something was up yesterday when they shoved that tube down my throat for a test."

Bird shuddered. "That must have hurt."

"Sort of. Afterward, I made my mother tell me what was going on." He looked out the window for a moment and then turned back to her. "Tell me what you think. Is it all over? When you're dead, you're dead?" He eased back onto his pillows and pulled the sheet up under his chin. "You get your chance here on earth? And that's it?"

Bird shifted uncomfortably in her chair. She didn't know what to say.

"If there's nothing else . . ."—Josh paused— "I'm not getting a very long chance." His head dropped down.

Bird desperately wanted to cheer him. "Maybe you come back again," she said.

Slowly, he looked up. "You think so?"

"My dad says Grandma Hildy is in me. I was born on her birthday. A week after she died."

"Wow. You could be her." Josh looked her over as if he might see some hint of another person.

"Or maybe you go right to heaven," she said.

"You believe there is one?"

Bird nodded. "I think so."

"What's it like? Summer at Whitefish all year long?" Josh stared upward. "To swim, you just dive from a cloud into the lake."

"Oooh, that sounds nice." They sat quietly, eyes closed, imagining it.

Their reverie was interrupted a moment later when Josh's parents appeared at the door. Josh looked up apprehensively. "Did you find out? Do I have AIDS?"

His mother settled on his bed and took his hands. She was smiling, and Bird could see the relief on her face. "The test came back negative. It's not PCP."

"Just regular old pneumonia," his father added, clapping his hands together. "You're getting better with the penicillin. In a few days, you should be able to come home."

Bird slumped back into the soft vinyl cushion. Thank God. Then she jumped up, threw her arms around Josh, and kissed him on the cheek. He grabbed her shoulders and dug his fingers in. Then he pulled away, embarrassed.

"Does this mean I have to go to school in the fall?" Josh asked.

"Of course," his mother answered.

He looked knowingly at Bird. She remembered

telling him she would transfer to his school. How were all those strangers going to like her, anyway? She pushed the thought away. Josh was going to start seventh grade like everyone else. That was all that counted.

Bird canoed across the velvet-smooth waters of Whitefish Lake the next morning as shrouds of mist swirled and evaporated into the sky. The slush of her j-stroke was the only sound she heard except for the caw of a faraway crow. The lake water splashed off her paddle, warmer on her skin than the brisk air.

Bird reached her destination, Ossaway Island, but did not land. It did not feel right to go ashore without Josh. Rounding the curve, she startled a double-crested cormorant. The bird dropped a fish into the shallows of the cattail marsh, soared up, and circled overhead, silently protesting the loss of its breakfast.

Bird rested the paddle on her lap as she gazed through the mist at the solitary island. Ossaway had always seemed mysterious and powerful, knowing all that had passed since the glaciers formed it eons ago. Could it tell her the future, as well? Bird stared and listened, but the island would not tell her what she wanted to know most. How long would Josh live?

"Carolina!" Elliot exclaimed as her canoe slid up on the sand. "What a nice surprise."

"What are you doing?" she asked, inspecting the pile of rocks stretching out into the water in front of his cabin.

"Building a jetty. As the waves come in, they'll wash sand onto our beach." Bird looked at the pebble-strewn shore between the jetty and the whitewashed dock. "Bill was supposed to help me, but I couldn't pry him away from his book."

"I'll help you," Bird said. She pulled off her sneakers and picked up a cantaloupe-sized rock, waded into the water, and tossed it onto the jetty with a splash.

"You're much better at this than Bill," he said. Together, they lifted a large stone and dropped it on the growing wall. They worked in silence for a few minutes and then, in a quiet voice, Elliot asked, "You doing okay?"

She looked up at him. "You mean about Josh?" Elliot nodded. "I feel better now that I know he's getting out."

"Me, too." He heaved another rock onto the jetty.

"Elliot?"

"Yes?"

"Do you have any friends with AIDS?"

"Not now. I did have one." Elliot paused. "But he died."

Bird searched for another stone. "How long does it take . . ."—the words stuck in her throat and she coughed—"to make you die?"

"Let's leave this for now," Elliot said, pointing at the jetty. He brushed the sand off a flat rock on shore and sat down. Bird dropped on her knees next to him, facing the quiet lake. "No one can say how long a person will live. My friend died quickly. But that was before they had any medicines."

Bird dug her fingers into the sand. The grit pushed up under her nails. "What about Josh?"

"It's better these days. Josh may live for years." Elliot searched her face. "But he may not."

"He could live to be a grown-up?"

"Yes."

"Could he get married?"

"If he wanted to. Bird, you don't have a crush on him, do you?" Elliot looked surprised.

Bird blushed. She didn't want to have a whole discussion about that. "He's my best friend," was all she answered. They sat for a time listening to the rhythmic lapping of the waves against the shore. "I'm going to his school next year."

"You are?"

Bird nodded. "He asked me to. He's afraid no one there will be friends with him."

"Because he's HIV-positive?"

She hesitated. "He thinks they'll say he's gay."

Elliot's eyes fell to the sand. His fingers clutched a stone, and he cast it deep into the lake. "Josh is probably right. They will say that. Only they won't use the word *gay*. They'll call him a fag or a fem. At least that's what they called me."

"That's so mean," Bird said.

"Yeah, it is. But Josh is tough. He'll cope. And he'll make friends. He always has before." Elliot studied her face. "You sure you want to change schools?"

"He's counting on me."

"Maybe too much."

She rocked back. "What do you mean?"

"Josh has to learn to make it on his own."

Bird felt a rush of desire to go to her own school. She imagined walking each day with Shawno and Jenny. They would laugh and talk. But hadn't the decision been made? She couldn't switch on him now. She suddenly ached to be near Josh. "I said I would go to his school."

Elliot nodded. "I don't mean to tell you what to do." He put his hand on Bird's shoulder. "I understand why you two would stick together next year."

Bird watched a distant boat speed across the lake. She stood up. They had talked long enough. "Should we move some more rocks?" she asked. "So your beach is extra-sandy next year?" Although, looking up and down the rocky shore, Bird thought it was doubtful.

As Bird paddled home that afternoon, she took solace in the fact that Josh might live to be a grown-up. That meant lots more summers together. Hopefully. And Josh could get married. Do I want him to marry me? Bird shook her head. But what if he marries someone else! That was no good, either. Maybe they would both stay single and live at the lake all year long.

As she landed the canoe, she felt a coolness, fall's first breath, on her cheeks and forearms. School would start soon. She closed her eyes, imagining the dusty smell of chalk-filled erasers. She could see wide packs of No. 2 pencils the color of a classroom floor. She imagined the fun of meeting at the water fountain to receive a note. But the images were out of focus, indistinct. Who was giving her the note? Was she at Josh's school or her own?

Chapter 12

Josh's discharge from the hospital was marked with such fanfare that Bird did not at first notice anything different about him. For the next few days, the white cabin he shared with Joe became the focus of life at Melody Shores, a combination sickroom and party central.

Josh's oldest sister, Lizbeth, and her twin daughters flew in from New York. The little girls filled the grounds with chirrupy voices. Josh gradually grew stronger, able to play with his nieces on the beach and fish with them from the end of the dock.

On Saturday night the Birdsongs hosted a wiener roast. It was Josh's first outing since he had come home from the hospital. He and Bird stuffed themselves with hot dogs. For dessert, they gobbled s'mores—chocolate with roasted marshmallows squished between graham crackers. Bird helped Lizbeth's girls make the melted sandwiches. "You're so good with the children," Bird's mother observed. I guess I am, thought Bird, pleased, as the little girls competed to sit on her lap.

When Lizbeth and her family went back east and the hubbub died down, Josh and Bird were on their own. That's when she started noticing the change in him. "Let's go out to the trampoline," Bird urged their first afternoon alone. She was lying at his feet on his bunk as he read a comic book—his third one since she got there. He didn't respond. "*Josh!* Do you want to?"

"Shhh! I'm trying to finish this."

"Come on. I want to do something."

"Okay, okay." Josh threw the comic down. "But not swimming."

They decided to go to Mill Pond. Bird measured

her pace as they crossed through the woods, but Josh had no trouble keeping up. When they arrived, she pulled off her shoes and waded in. "Aren't you coming?" she asked.

"Nah," he answered, dropping onto the ground.

Later, Bird grew sweaty as they sat in the hot afternoon sun. "I'm boiling," she said. "Let's go in the lake."

"I *told* you I don't want to go swimming. Jump in the pond if you're so hot." Bird waded back in, using all her self-control not to splash him.

The next day, after much coaxing, Josh agreed to put on his bathing suit. Bird waited for him down at the beach. What was taking so long? Finally, he stepped out of the equipment cabin, his old underwater mask dangling from one arm. He walked slowly down to the lake. "Is it cold?"

Bird flipped a stream of water back at him. "Check it out."

"Stop it!" he yelled, retreating to a lawn chair.

Bird fell into the embracing softness of the water. "Come in, Josh. It feels so good."

He did, finally, staying inside the L-shaped dock,

exploring underwater life in the shallows. Bird started for the trampoline once. "Stay with me!" Josh commanded. She did, all the while longing to swim underwater laps again.

Later that week, on a breezy evening, Josh and Bird fished on the far side of Ossaway. The nights were chillier now as fall crept closer. Josh reeled in his line. "Let's go, Bird. I'm cold."

"But we just got here." Last night it was the same thing. She had to talk him into going, and then he wanted to leave right away. "How will we ever catch anything?"

"Who cares if we do?"

"What about the contest?"

"We'll never win." Josh put away his Rapala lure and slammed the lid of the tackle box. "It's a stupid contest, anyway."

Bird gave him a skeptical look. "So, what's with you?" she asked, irritation creeping into her voice.

His eyes flashed. "I'm cold. That's all. You got a problem with that?" He yanked the starter cord. The motor coughed. He squeezed the bulb on the gas line. Josh pulled again. The motor just sputtered. He tried again. Nothing. "This hunk of junk!" He slugged the engine. Josh yanked back his hand. "Ouch!"

"Are you okay?"

He rubbed his fingers. "We're stuck here."

"Maybe it's flooded." They sat in silence waiting for the gasoline to trickle out of the engine.

"I'm not going fishing anymore," Josh told her. "I've had it."

"Oh, Josh." Bird groaned. He wouldn't swim laps anymore. He wasn't going to fish anymore. He was giving up on everything. The buzz of an engine made Bird turn. Scotty Kovacs, who lit off the Fourth of July fireworks, was racing toward them. He pulled up alongside them and grabbed on. The two fishing boats rocked side by side in the choppy water.

"Won't it start?" he asked.

Josh gave the cord a hard jerk. A promising sputter. Again. The engine roared to life.

"There you go," Scotty said. "Hey, you guys want to come over tomorrow night?"

"And do what?" Josh asked.

"Build rockets. With my fireworks club."

Josh turned to Bird. "You want to?" She agreed, even though she didn't give two hoots about making fireworks.

"Telephone," Bird's father called out the back door the next day. "It's Josh." He called her every morning now.

"When are you coming over?" he asked.

"In a little while," she replied. "But, Josh, I can't go to Scotty's tonight."

"You have to."

"My mother won't let me."

"Why not? I'm not going alone."

"We're visiting her clients on Gull Lake. For dinner."

"Stay here. You can eat at my house."

"No. I have to meet their kids. Josh, why won't you go to Scotty's alone?"

But he didn't answer. Bird listened to the dial tone. He had hung up.

* * *

119

After Bird finished a toasted cheese sandwich with her dad the next day, she canoed over to Josh's. She was determined to get him out to the trampoline. She found him in the grass behind the main cabin. "How was last night?" she asked. "Did you go to Scotty's?"

Josh shook his head. "Didn't feel like it."

Bird collapsed to the ground. Why in the world wouldn't he go without her? Elliot was right. He did rely on her too much.

As she lay there, a red convertible barreled up the driveway. *Hoo-haw, hoo-haw,* sounded the horn, bringing Joe out of the cabin. The car lurched to a stop, and Ginny Gage stepped out.

She waved to Joe. "My father finally let me drive it. And some bozo in Pequot Lakes almost sideswiped me." She slammed the door. "Know what my father would do if I scratched his car?"

"What?" Bird called out, curious to know the answer.

Ginny ignored her. She slid her long fingers over the shiny fender and looked up at Joe. "Want to drive it?"

"Yes! Come here for a minute." The two of them went inside.

Bird turned to Josh. "Did you hear that?"

"What?"

"About her almost getting sideswiped. Remember that sticker I gave you? It's perfect."

"She'll see us," Josh said.

"No she won't. She's busy with Joe."

"Think we should?"

"Are you crazy? Hurry."

"Okay, okay." Bird followed him to his cabin. Inside, Josh pulled a large yellow bag out from under his bed and dumped the contents on the floor: smoke bombs, a fake melted Fudgsicle, exploding matches, bullet-hole decals, and a fake arm. He pawed through it all and pulled out the fender bender sticker. They ran back to the roadster. He peeled the backing from the sticker and plastered it onto the car door. "Now, we tell her," Josh said.

They found Ginny sitting at the kitchen table with Joe, who was finishing a piece of lemon meringue pie. "Are you sure that guy didn't hit you?" Josh asked her.

"What do you mean?"

"There's an awful bad scratch on the door."

"You're lying." Ginny jumped out of her chair so fast it fell over. She reached the screen door and threw it open. There was a moment of dead silence, and then her scream pierced the air.

"Didn't I tell you?" Josh asked, standing at her elbow.

Ginny flew down the steps. Josh and Joe and Bird bounded down behind her. "I'll be grounded for a year!" she shouted, racing across the lawn to the car. "My father will kill me." When Ginny reached the convertible, she stooped and ran her fingers over the plastic decal. Then she cried out again in a lower, more ominous tone.

For the first time since he had gotten out of the hospital, Josh was laughing. He had fallen to the ground, his whole body quivering in the grass. Bird whooped alongside him.

Ginny, not having noticed Josh's moodiness, didn't care that the joke had cheered him. She stormed toward them. "You little brats. I've had enough. You think it's funny?"

Josh looked at Bird and they burst into more raucous giggles. Joe started chuckling, too, and Ginny turned her icy stare on him. "Don't encourage them," she snapped.

"Oh, Ginny. Relax. You've got to admit it was a good trick."

This enraged her more. "Is that what you think? Well! You need to grow up if you want to go out with me." She marched toward the car and then spun back to face him. "I don't date boys. I date men." She got in, revved the engine, and tore out of the driveway, scrape decal and all.

Her sudden departure quieted Josh and Bird. Joe stared after her shaking his head. "Geez! Can't take a joke." Then his gaze fell on the perpetrators. "Whose bright idea was it?" He lunged toward his brother. "As if I didn't know."

Josh pointed at Bird. "It was her. It was, I swear." Joe started tickling his little brother's stomach. "Stop!" Josh begged as he writhed in laughter.

Joe finally let him go. "I was all set to take a spin in that car."

Josh sat up. "We could go swimming instead."

"Hmm. Out to the diving platform?" Joe asked.

"Yes!" Bird shouted.

"Okay," Josh reluctantly agreed.

Down at the beach, they waded out to the end of the dock. "Here, Josh, get on my shoulders," Joe instructed. "See how far we can walk." Josh climbed up on his brother, and they went deeper and deeper. The water reached Josh's armpits before the buoyancy of it lifted him off. He stroked the rest of the way to the trampoline.

"Let's do laps," Bird encouraged him.

"I don't want to."

"Just a few."

"No."

Joe sat on the platform just above them, his feet hanging into the water. "Go on, Josh."

"What if it makes me sick?" He gripped the ladder with both hands.

"You can do two," Bird urged.

"Will you follow me?" he asked. They took deep breaths, submerged, and swam slowly to the far opening. One. Bird thought he was going to bolt for the surface, but he pulled himself around and went back the other way. Two. Josh didn't come up for air. He pulled through and shot back toward the other end. They did three. And then four. Josh's head popped out of the water and he clutched the ladder, choking a little. "See, I did it," Josh told them. "Now don't bug me anymore, okay?"

When Bird was ready to leave for home that evening, Josh grabbed her by the shoulder. "Maybe we should go fishing in the morning. Try that weedy spot where you and Joe caught so many."

It was a flash of the old Josh. "Yes," she cried. She wasn't going to give him a chance to change his mind. "We have to leave really early. Don't eat breakfast. I'll bring peanut butter and mayonnaise sandwiches."

Josh and Bird set off the next morning in the pinkish yellow blush of first sunlight. As they neared the mouth of the Pine River, Josh cut the motor and let his line out. The boat glided into the weeds.

Bird sat still. The bossy nagging of the engine

bounced off the lake and landed muffled in the conifers standing above. Then she could hear nothing but the morning quiet. The splish of a frog as it jumped in the drink. The whizzing of a dragonfly circling over the lake. The gurgling song of a purple martin. *Tchew-wew. Tchew-wew.* Bird closed her eyes and faced up into the sun, relishing the peaceful moment.

Her thoughts drifted until she heard a whisper. "Bird!" Her eyes snapped open. "Bird, something's nibbling." Josh held his rod still and then jerked it high into the air. "I hooked one," he cried. He was gripping the rod with both hands, its tip bowed toward the lake. He struggled to wind in.

"Go easy," Bird advised. "Don't let it snap your line."

Josh dipped his pole and let some line out. Then he began cranking in again. He turned the reel slowly, his knuckles white from the grip. Suddenly, the line went slack. "Oh no," Bird cried. "Did it break?"

"I can't tell," Josh answered. There was a splash not more than an oar's length from the boat. The majestic tail of the huge fish rose out of the water. Bird clapped her hands to her face. *The giant muskie!* Josh's fishing line snapped taut again. The force of it yanked him halfway over the side of the boat. "Help, Bird!" he cried.

Chapter 13

*"Lean away!" Bird shouted. The muskie was run-*ning now. Its powerful surge pulled Josh ever clos-er to the water. He struggled to keep his balance and hold onto the pole.

"Get over here," he yelled to Bird.

"Don't let go," she called, scrambling across the seats to the back of the boat.

Josh was being lifted off his seat; his upper torso drew nearer and nearer the lake. Would the muskie attack if he fell in? "Hold me, Bird. Pull me down." She grabbed Josh's waist and clasped her hands tight over his stomach. The pull against her was intense. She could feel his chest heaving as he sucked in breath and blew out. "He's too strong, Bird."

"You're stronger," she shouted, clutching his belly. Her cheek pressed hard against his back. She could feel him, lank and bony, straining with all his might. "I love you, Josh," she cried out.

"Uunh!" he grunted. His body shifted back into her grip. They gained leverage. He wound the reel once and then again. He cranked, slowly, and then, while the muskie rested, faster like he was winding a yo-yo.

Without warning, the fish charged again, like an ocean liner, yanking Josh toward the lake. He started to slip from her grasp. "Feed him line," she yelled.

Josh released a few yards. The pole jumped like a spring. It bowed again when he stopped more line from escaping. "My fingers," he moaned.

"Hold on!"

Josh clung fast. He rode out the surge and began reeling in. "I want this sucker!"

When the muskie rested, he spun the reel, closing the gap. He held on through two more runs, winding rapidly when he had the chance. At last, the fish surfaced, longer than a small shark, with teeth almost as sharp. "Look at it!" Josh exclaimed. The muskellunge seemed to peer back at them with its glassy yellow-and-black eyes.

Bird grabbed the net and jabbed it into the water. She worked it underneath the glistening fish, dark green and white with yellowish fins. As she slowly lifted, the supple muskie flipped out of the net, splashing back into the lake. The spray lashed Bird's face and she jumped back. Her heart skipped a beat. Was it gone?

Josh raised the muskie to the surface again. "Yahoo!" he shouted, dancing on the seat, as Bird hauled it safely into the boat. They laid it on the floor between the two forward-most seats. It thrashed violently. When it rested, Josh held its head flat with his foot while he removed the lure. Then he collapsed onto his seat, next to the motor, arms sprawled on either side of him. "We did it," he said between breaths. She squeezed onto the seat next to his feet, flushed with excitement. He sighed. "We did it."

Josh rested a moment and then sat up. "Bird?"

He peered at her with intense eyes. Oh no, here it comes. Why had she bared her soul to him? He was going to ask what she meant. She waited as he formed the thought. "Did you bring those sandwiches? *I'm starving!*"

She retrieved the crinkled brown lunch bag stowed in the bow, slid out two well-slathered sandwiches, and handed him one. They wolfed them down, tangy and sweet, until their mouths were thick with peanut butter. "Joo bring milg?" he asked. She shook her head.

Josh shrugged, leaned over the oarlock, and dunked his face into the lake. Bird climbed next to him and plunged her head in, too. He turned to her in the underwater sunlight. Ever so slowly, he slid his hand down her forehead, nose, lips, and chin. A shiver went up her warm back.

Then their heads burst out of the water. Was the giant muskie really lying in their boat? Yes. In all its glory. Josh splashed water on the fish. Then he put two fingers in his mouth and let loose an ear-piercing whistle. As he drove them home, Josh turned the motor crazily, tilting the boat this way and that. Bird laughed into the wind streaming past both sides of her face. Whitefish Lake had never looked so sparkling blue.

Back at Melody Shores, Josh fit a stringer hook in the muskie's mouth and hung it into the lake off a dock pole. Then he retrieved an inflatable pool out of the equipment cabin. They washed the cobwebs off it and took turns blowing it up. Josh nestled it into the floor of the boat and ladled water into it until it was half full. "You can breathe in here," Josh said to the muskie as he lifted it into the pool. The muskie righted itself immediately.

Josh led Bird up the hill to the old, black dinner bell. The cabins were all still. Josh grabbed the wood handle and pulled down hard. *Bong*. "You're gonna wake everyone," Bird whispered.

"I'm trying to."

Bird grabbed the other handle and they rang it together. *Bong. Bong. Bong.*

Josh's father appeared in the doorway, clutching his pajama bottoms at the waist. "What is it, Josh?" he asked, squinting into the morning sun.

"Dad, wait till you see it!"

"See what?" Mr. Charkey opened the door and started toward them. "Get Mom," Josh commanded.

Bong. Bong. Bong. Joe stumbled out into the daylight in rumpled gym shorts, his hair mashed all to one side.

"What's going on?"

"You'll see."

When Josh's mother arrived in her flowered bathrobe and thongs, they all trooped single file down the path to the beach. "This better be good," Joe hollered from the rear. "Or you're going for a swim."

Josh marched to the end of the dock where his boat was tethered and pointed down at his catch. "Ta-da!"

Joe jumped into the boat and touched the tail of the fish. "You caught it?" He stared up at his brother, amazed. "The giant muskie."

"We caught it together. I couldn't have done it without Bird."

"Josh!" Bird exclaimed. "I just held you down. *You* caught it."

Mrs. Charkey clapped her hands together. "This calls for a party. Who wants waffles?"

"With blueberry syrup?" Josh asked.

"And fresh whipped cream," Mrs. Charkey

answered as she led the way off the dock. "Get your sister up. How on earth could she sleep through that clanging?"

After breakfast, it was time for the official weighing at Breezy Woods. Bird took the motor, running them the long way around Ossaway Island. "Look!" Josh called to her as they came around the bend. Irv LeBeck was fishing in his usual spot. Bird idled the throttle as the boat glided up behind him. "You still in first?" Josh asked.

"Of course. Nobody can touch me." He drained the last swallow from a beer can and crumpled it in his fist. "I'm gonna get me a water bed with the winnings."

Bird could just imagine him sprawled on one. "I wouldn't count on it," she said knowingly.

At that moment, Josh hauled the stringer out of the pool and lifted the muskie high with both arms. "How much does it weigh, Irv?" he shouted, giving a little shake with his pelvis. "Hit it, Bird!" She gassed the engine and they roared off, leaving Irv dazed in a wake of bubbles.

As they held onto the dock at Breezy Woods

waiting for Mr. Carlson to come and weigh the muskie, Bird stuffed one hand into her pocket. Oh! She had forgotten that she brought it. She jerked out the heavy coin. "Look!"

"Your silver dollar," Josh said. "You had it along this morning?" Bird nodded. He laughed and gave it a kiss.

"My aunt wasn't kidding," Bird said. "It is lucky!"

"Yeah! Let's take it to Vegas."

Mr. Carlson called to them as he neared the dock. "Let's see what you got." Josh hoisted the stringer. "Whoa, mama!" He hooked a scale into the mouth of the fish. "Nineteen pounds, eleven ounces," he announced as he held the muskie by its gills. "Amazing!" They were in first place by more than ten pounds. He posed Josh on the end of the dock and snapped photographs. "Smile. This one's going on the front page."

"Take one with Bird, too," Josh told him. "I couldn't have done it without her." Bird wished he would stop saying that.

"What are you going to do with it?" Mr. Carlson asked as he focused the camera on both of them.

"It'd look great over the fireplace." Bird glanced at Josh. She knew the muskie would never hang above a mantel.

Back in the boat, Bird's eyes fell on the cartoon drawings on the inflatable pool wedged between the seats. She remembered the day she had cut her thumb in that pool. Josh had served her tea and a grass sandwich. They had always taken care of each other. And now, she couldn't believe what she was thinking. Was she going to shove him away when he needed her most? Was she going to tell him to start Madison without her?

The weeds brushed against the sides of the boat as they glided toward the mouth of the Pine River. Josh took the stringer hook out of the muskie's lip. Then he and Bird lifted one side of the pool, spilling the water into the lake. When it was almost empty, they turned it up and the muskie flopped back into Whitefish Lake. With one sweep of its grand tail, it disappeared. Josh beamed. "Wait until we tell the kids at school about this."

Chapter 14

*Josh jammed two fingers in his mouth and whis-*tled as he dropped Bird on the end of her dock. "Come over later," he said. "We've got to decide how to spend the prize money."

She nodded and waved him off. But she had other things on her mind. The last days of summer were slipping away like a rope sliding through her hands. Was she starting seventh grade with Josh or not?

She heard the murmur of voices from inside the Birdsong cottage as she loped up the hill. "Guess what?" she called from outside the screen door. No answer. She found them in her bedroom setting up *her* old crib. "What are you doing?"

"Getting ready for next year," her father answered. "We'll have Amanda with us in the spring."

She looked at her mother sponging down the yellow rail cushion. Her firm, mounded belly pushed out of a purple T-shirt. "But that's my crib."

"Honey, you don't need it anymore," said her mother.

Of course she didn't. But some things—like her first bed, for heaven's sake—were special. They just took it. "You didn't even ask me."

"We're asking you now," her father said. "How about it?" Bird hesitated.

"It needs paint," said her mother. "You can touch it up."

Bird loved to paint. "Well, I suppose."

"Good," said her father.

"Don't you want to hear what happened today?" Bird asked.

"Sure we do," he replied. He lowered himself

onto the floor and slid his body under the crib to inspect the latch.

Bird stamped her foot. "Dad! You're not listening."

He rolled his head back and looked at her upside down. "Sure I am."

"Go on," said her mother.

"Josh caught the giant muskie!"

Her father tried to sit up and clunked his head on the bed rails. "No!"

"Swear to God. I had to hold him down or the darn thing woulda dunked him."

Her father slid out from under the bed and clambered to his feet. "Did you weigh in?"

"Almost twenty pounds," Bird crowed. "Josh clinched first."

Her mother rubbed her bare arms as if a shiver had just run through her. "He must be thrilled."

"Tell us everything," her father demanded. Bird gladly did so, acting out the most exciting moments.

Afterward, she went outside and climbed along the wooded bluff overhanging the lake. A brisk wind had come up, and Bird raised her arms letting it blow against her like she was a sail. The softness of it against her cheeks reminded her of Josh's touch that morning as he had gently stroked her face underwater. Slowly, Bird closed her arms around her chest. Her eyes welled up with tears. "Don't let go," she whispered. "Josh, don't leave me."

Brushing at her eyes, Bird stumbled back underneath two old knobby pines and fell onto a cushion of needles the color of ground cinnamon. A frightened daddy longlegs rushed away. She listened as the trees groaned and chatted in the wind high above her.

What if she didn't go to Josh's school? When would she see him? At parties. Sometimes on Saturdays. Less than an hour had passed since he had dropped her off, and already she missed him. How would she get through the months until next summer?

Bird lay there so absorbed that the daddy longlegs decided it was safe to climb across her arm. Bird's wrist tickled, she looked, and then flailed her arm to shake the thing off. "I'm trying to think," she scolded as it raced away again.

Bird tried to imagine what seventh grade would be like. She knew that it was different. You weren't in grade school anymore, which had a kindergarten, for Pete's sake. There would be homework and real marks: A's, B's, and C's. And dances. Jenny was always practicing in front of the mirror for the seventh grade dances. Did Josh dance? Would they go together? Would they do everything together?

At Longfellow, she'd know half the school. There would be friends to walk with every day. At Madison, she wouldn't know anyone but Josh. Would she fit in there?

Bird struggled to figure out what she wanted. She couldn't make up her mind about anything anymore. It wasn't just school, but Amanda, too. There was a crib taking up half her room. Did she want a sister or not?

She pushed herself up into a sitting position and shook the clash of thoughts out of her head. I have to decide about Josh. She looked up into the cone-laden boughs. "Should I switch to his school?" She took a deep breath and slowly blew out. From somewhere inside her, the answer came.

"Did ya see the look on Irv's face?" Josh asked as they sat together at Breathtaking View. "You coulda popped an egg in his mouth." He leaned back on his arms, surveying the lake where he was now Fishing King. Down the way, the cables on a sailboat rang hard against the mast, as if to sound his victory.

"You whomped everyone," Bird said. "What're you gonna get with the money?"

Josh scrunched up his face and looked skyward. "I don't know. Maybe a thousand candy bars."

"Take a long time to eat that many."

"I've got time," he said quietly.

She sat up on her knees and sucked in some of the wind tousling her hair. "Can you believe it? School starts in two weeks."

"I'm trying not to think about it."

"Could you? Just for a minute? I have to tell you something."

"What?"

"I'm afraid you'll be mad."

"Tell me!"

Bird's throat tightened. "I'm not going to Madison."

"You're not?" Josh's eyes flashed.

"I changed my mind."

"Biiiirrrrrd. *Please.*"

"You don't need me there, Josh."

He turned away and picked up a pinecone. One by one, he plucked the seeds out of it and threw them over the bluff. They were caught by the wind and blown out over the whitecapping lake. Bird tried to find his eyes, but he kept them fixed on Whitefish. "Why'd you change your mind?" he finally asked.

"We're so close," she said.

"So?"

"It might be better if we went to different schools."

"Why?"

"Because."

"That's not an answer." His voice rose above the rush of the wind. "Because *why*?" He glared.

She couldn't think of what to say. "Because you

wouldn't build fireworks without me," she blurted out. "You won't do anything without me."

He flinched, and she saw the wounded look in his eyes. Josh scrambled to his feet and threw the dismembered cone over the bluff. "You gave me your word!" He turned away.

"Josh. Wait." He headed up the hill. "Where are you going?" she called after him. He marched to his cabin and slammed the screen door without a glance back. Her shoulders slumped. She wanted to roll off the cliff and crash to the beach below. She had just betrayed her best friend.

Bird jabbed the paddle into the water with quick, short strokes. She had let Josh alone for a day. Now she wanted to talk, to put what had happened behind them.

As she neared the dock at Melody Shores, she glimpsed Josh through the trees, descending the hill. He looked up and froze. Then he pivoted and rushed back up the hill. What was Josh doing? He must have seen her. Bird's face turned red and hot. He's running away from me!

Should I go after him? "No," she said aloud. She

was not going to make a fool out of herself by chasing him. She remembered the time when some girls from school had ditched her on their bikes. She had tried to catch up until one shouted, "Ride away!" They left Bird standing there straddling her bicycle, humiliated. And now Josh had made her feel the same way. She turned the canoe 180 degrees and paddled furiously across the lake toward home, her eyes burning. I'm never going over there again!

Chapter 15

Bird twisted her hair around one finger as she stared out the picture window, haunted by her decision not to go to Josh's school. She had not seen him for three days. Bird edged toward the phone to call him, but stopped midstep. What if he said he was busy? Or worse. Hung up. She turned to the cupboard and found an old box of saltines. They were stale, but she ate them anyway, without butter or jam.

I'm glad we had a fight, she thought. I'm tired of worrying. Tired of him being sick. Her stomach twinged, and she pressed her hand to her belly.

"What's wrong?" her mother asked, coming in from the garden.

She let her hand drop. "Nothing."

"Aren't you going to Josh's today?"

"No." Bird fell into the swivel rocker and opened a magazine.

"You spending the rest of summer indoors?"

"If I feel like it."

Brrrringgg. Brrringgg. The phone on the wall jangled. Bird jumped up and ran for it. Maybe it was Josh. "Hello," she said softly.

Music and a recording. "You may already have won . . ." Bird slammed the phone down.

"Ouch!" Bird knocked her funny bone on the crib while changing into her pajamas that night. It's too crowded in here. She shoved the crib, making the lambs on the mobile dance. Bird crawled into bed. Mad at herself. Mad at the world.

That night she dreamed that Roxie, the golden retriever up at the farm, gave birth to puppies. One was sick and Mr. Burkett gave it to Bird, wrapped in an old towel. She kept it warm and played music for it. Soft, sweet notes. She awakened. There *was* music playing. Bird grabbed her flashlight, hopped out of bed, and shined it all around. Ah-ha! The mobile. She poked it. A few more notes rang out.

In the secret stillness of the middle of night, Bird shined her flashlight into the crib. Two yellow cotton blankets, neatly folded, rested on the mattress. A stuffed monkey stood in the corner. She stretched, but couldn't reach it. Bird pressed her belly against the side rail, pushed up with her arms, and tumbled into the crib. Hugging the monkey to her, she wound the mobile. Then she lay her head down on the soft covers. The melody was so familiar, one her mother used to sing: "Hush little baby, now don't you cry." It lulled her to sleep.

CRACK! The brace under the frame gave way. CRASH! One end of the mattress collapsed onto the floor. Shaken out of a sound sleep, Bird's eyes flew open. It was morning. Her body slid slowly down the incline, and her shoulders hit the floor with a bump. Good grief! She had fallen asleep in Amanda's crib.

"What was that?" her father yelled from the living room. She heard his running steps and then her door burst open. *"Bird!"*

What could she say? "'Morning, Dad." She inched across the floor on her back, stood, and brushed off the dust. "Lucky that didn't happen when Amanda was in there."

He looked at her in disbelief. "Go get my toolbox."

"What happened?" Bird's mother rushed in from outside. "Are you all right?" Bird nodded. She went off for the tools, came back, and gave them to her father.

While he repaired the broken crib, Bird and her mother went outside and sat on the wooden deck steps. "Are you still upset," her mother asked, "that we're having another child?"

What did she think? That Bird had gotten into the crib trying to be their baby again? "Mom! I was just fooling around in there." Bird dropped her eyes. She could feel her mother's gaze on her.

"You know," she said, brushing her finger across

Bird's cheek, "we'll love you more than ever when Amanda gets here."

Bird sat silently, soaking in the words. Was that possible? That there would be more love, not less, because of Amanda? Her mother *had* been different lately. She worked less and had more time for Bird. (And she had gotten awfully good at back rubs.)

"Come on," said her mother, "let's make breakfast for your father." She cooked scrambled eggs with mushrooms and Swiss cheese. Bird fixed jasmine tea for her parents, with cream the way they liked it. She had a cup, too, with three spoonfuls of sugar in it.

That afternoon, Bird's father found her sitting on the hood of the car. He went in the basement and came out dribbling a basketball. "How 'bout a game of horse?" He was trying to be nice, so she played, but she wanted to be out on the lake with Josh. "Give me a rematch," he said when she beat him. Bird shook her head and wandered off.

From the distant woods came the sputtering *rat-a-tat-tat* of a package of firecrackers lit all at once. She remembered the look on Ginny's face when Josh had exploded one underneath her. She loved the stir he caused. No one could play tricks like Josh.

Dinner came and went. Bird lay on the couch staring at the knotholes in the ceiling. The moon had not yet risen, and the darkness outside pressed in on her. Would they go back to the city without speaking? Could they? She missed him so much her sides ached. She grabbed the sofa cushion and pulled it down over her face.

Chuga-chuga-chuga. She heard a motor down on the lake. "Who's that?" she asked, jumping up and going to the window.

"Fisherman," her father answered as he read, one leg slung over the arm of the chair.

Out on the stoop, Bird peered through the darkness. A fishing boat was cruising back and forth in front of their dock. Could it be? This late? Bird tore down the hill. From shore, she could see. She drew her hands to her chest. It was Josh.

She waved. He turned the nose of the boat toward her and shot the back end around. The stained wood of the dock groaned as the bow scraped against it. Josh's face was illuminated in the glow from the pole light. "Come with me," he said.

"Where?"

"Out on the lake." He stared up at her, fidgeting with the splayed end of the tie rope.

"I'll just tell my dad."

She was back in a moment and stepped into the boat, choosing the middle seat, nearer him. He gunned the throttle and they roared off. In the middle of Whitefish Lake, he cut the engine and they sliced a path through the now-silent night. Millions of stars, each a mere needle prick of light, spilled from the blackness.

"You're not still mad?" she asked quietly.

Josh shoved the red gas can so that it was balanced in the center of the boat. "Who says I'm not?"

"You came to get me."

"Why didn't *you* come to *my* house?"

Bird bristled. "I did. You ran away."

Josh scuffed at some fish scales crusted on the boat bottom. "I didn't know what to do. Just took off." He gulped. "I waited and waited for you to come again."

"I didn't know." Why hadn't she gone after him that day!

"I couldn't tell you." He looked up into the sky, and tears began running over the tip of his ear into his hair. "I wanted to show you. I'm okay on my own." He drew in a jagged breath.

Bird's eyes welled up. "Oh, Josh." She reached for him. When she hooked his finger, he let out a groan and began crying in heaving sobs. She jumped to his seat and grabbed his arm in both her hands. "What is it?"

Josh's body shook. "I don't want . . ." He began sobbing harder. "I don't want . . . to die alone." His body convulsed and Bird pulled him to her. He cried and cried, his head resting hard on her chest.

"Josh, . . . Josh." She wrapped him tightly in her arms. Gradually, his body relaxed and his sobbing stopped. Only his heavy breathing could be heard in the quiet night. As they drifted on the water, the waxing moon, luminous and yellow, pushed its way into the dark sky.

After a time, Josh snuffled and sat up, wiping the tears and sweat off his hot face. He stood and peeled off his shirt. "I'm going in." Before Bird could stop him—they weren't supposed to swim alone at night—he had kicked off his shoes and perched on the side of the boat in just shorts. Josh sprang up with such force that the boat tossed from side to side. He rose up in an arc and, with arms outstretched before him, dived into the moon's yellow light spilling across the lake.

As Bird watched him disappear into the water, she remembered the way he had described heaven that day in the hospital. Summer at Whitefish all year long. To swim, you would just dive from a cloud.

Josh surfaced and rolled over on his back. With frog kicks, he propelled himself around in a circle. Then he lifted himself into the boat and tumbled onto the floor, dripping. He looked up at Bird tenderly, unembarrassed. She had never felt so close to him. Her lower lip trembled and she bit it. "Don't feel bad," he said. "I'm okay now."

She threw back her head, willing herself not to cry. Shaking, she forced a laugh. "Guess what? Last night, I slept in Amanda's crib."

"C'mon," he said, incredulous.

"It broke. Crashed to the floor with me in it."

Josh laughed. "What were you doing in there?"

Bird scooted forward so she could lie back on her seat and gaze at the Milky Way. "Remembering."

Josh pulled on his shirt, propped a cushion under his head, and stretched out on the floor. Out in the middle of Whitefish Lake, nothing obstructed their view of the expanse. As they drifted, a shooting star blazed across the sky, its bright tail fading behind it. Bird closed her eyes and wished for a cure for AIDS.

When her lids opened, Josh was lying on his side looking at her. "Ready to go?" he asked.

"I'm tired." He sat up. "We gotta get up early tomorrow."

"We do?"

"Yup. There's only a week of summer left. We can't waste a minute."

* * *

155

In each of the days that followed, Bird arrived at Melody Shores just after dawn. She and Josh seined for minnows with an old bedsheet. They caught so many that Josh made a LIVE BAIT sign, and they taped it to the bench on the end of the dock. Fishing boats stopped, and Josh and Bird sold their catch.

"My dad brought up a letter from school," Josh told her one afternoon as they sat on either side of the sign. Minnows swam in pails at their feet "I got assigned to the computer lab."

"What's that?"

"This special section. You learn everything from computers."

"You don't have books?"

"Nope. I'll go there for math, science, and independent study." A fisherman went by and Josh pointed to their sign, but he didn't stop. "You know what my independent study's going to be? Computer games."

Bird laughed. "Will they let you?"

"Why not?"

"I don't think they have anything like that at my school," Bird said.

"See. You should go to Madison." Josh flashed a look at her. "Just kidding."

She wondered. "Do you still mind?"

Josh stared out over the lake and then looked at her. "Well, maybe a little. But, geez, I'm almost twelve. No one has to take care of me anymore." Josh slipped his toes out of his thongs and sat on his feet. "Besides, it might have spoiled things. You know." He pointed at himself and then at Bird. "You and me." Though it was a sweltering hot day, a shiver ran through her.

As they sat there, Joe came running down the hill. "Watch this," he said. He leaned off the end of the dock and fell, face forward, into the water.

"The dog days of August," Mrs. Charkey told them as she dragged a lawn chair knee deep into Whitefish and dropped into it. "Thank heaven for the lake." Josh and Bird gave up on selling minnows and got their air mattresses. Racing, they propelled themselves out past the diving platform. "That's far enough," Josh's mother shouted.

"Look." Bird pointed. Ginny roared by them in her father's runabout. The wake washed in and they rode it on their rafts. "She called Joe, you know," Josh said, grinning impishly.

"She did?"

"Said she was ready to forgive him."

Bird flipped over on her mattress, giggling. "How 'bout us?"

Josh gave her a conspiratorial look. Then he lurched his belly forward, off the mattress. "Here goes," he called, lining up before the cross-boards of the diving platform.

"Wait." Bird paddled with her hands over to him. "What'd he tell her?"

Josh raised his eyebrows high. "Said he's busy. For the rest of the summer." Bird looked up and saw Joe lazily sunning his muscled chest on the end of the dock. "You think she got the message?" Josh asked.

Bird glanced at the disappearing boat. "She's still riding by here." Josh snorted and began breathing deeply in preparation for laps. Bird knew he tested himself this way to prove he was still strong. He plunged below. She raised up on her elbows, counting. He was under a long time, a good sign.

"I did it," he shouted as his curly hair burst above the waters of Whitefish. "I did nine."

"Use the ratchet head," Bird's father called to the worker who had come down from Burkett Farm to help take out the dock. Bird swallowed hard as she and Josh watched this Labor Day ritual. The man fitted the wrench and waded out chest deep. He spun the bolts, loosening them from their clamps. Section by section, the two men lifted the dock off its poles and stacked it in pieces on the sand, dismantling summer.

She and Josh walked to the cabin, past the vegetable garden, its fruits stripped and the plants plowed under. A bushel of green tomatoes for pickling sat on the steps. Inside, Bird's mother was emptying the refrigerator.

"Here." She handed them a pint of ice cream, half full. "Finish this, you two." They took two spoons and devoured it.

"Anything else, Mom?"

"There's some leftover three-bean salad." They hustled outside. "Don't go far. We'll be ready to leave soon," she called after them. Ready? Bird wasn't ready.

Down at the beach, she saw the canoe. "C'mon." They paddled out, heading up toward Breezy Woods. The bluff alongside them was dotted with red oak trees, their pointed leaves tinged with crimson.

"Tomorrow at this time I'll be in math class," Bird moaned.

"Not me," said Josh. Madison started a day later.

"On Wednesday, then."

"Nope. I'll be in the computer lab."

"You luck." He seemed okay about school. But was she?

"Carolina!" Her father yelled from shore. "Come on, now. We're trying to close up." The sinking feeling inside her grew stronger. "This goes in the garage," he said when they landed. He and Josh carried the canoe up, and she followed with the paddles. On their way back to the beach, Bird saw that all the shades in the cabin were pulled down tight.

They skipped rocks in silence. "Your parents are almost ready," Josh said. "I'm gonna take off." He shrugged and smiled at her, his green baseball cap on backward.

Her eyes misted up. No. No. It was too soon. Then it hit her. Smack! Like the sting of the water when she did a belly flop off the water trampoline. Elliot thought Josh relied on her too much. Really, it was the other way around!

She could not say good-bye to him. Bird turned and bolted up the hill. "Wait, Josh!" she cried. "Don't go." She fled into the cabin. From her bedroom window, she saw her parents packing the car. She collapsed onto her bunk. Was it too late to change schools? How could she get along without Josh?

She knew he was waiting down at the beach. But she lay there, lonely and ashamed of her helplessness. In the tiny room, her eyes stared straight into the crib. A play of light spilled over the yellow covers. Amanda would be born soon. Bird went to the crib, reached down, and rubbed her fingers along the soft, satin edge of the blanket. She closed her eyes. It was time to go.

She couldn't keep Josh waiting any longer. She had to say good-bye. But not without giving him something of hers to take with him. Bird's eyes shot open. She yanked open her packed suitcase, rifled through it, and found what she wanted. Then she hurried down to the beach.

"Where did you go?" Josh asked.

"To get something for you." She opened her palm and showed him the 1921 Liberty dollar. "Here."

"You can't give this away. It's your lucky dollar."

"Take it," she said, pressing it into his palm. Her eyes welled up.

"Hey," he said as he took the coin. "You'll be at my birthday party. In two weeks."

Bird rubbed her face with the back of her hand. "Know what you want?"

Josh looked up into the sky. "Maybe some fishing lures." Tears rolled down Bird's cheeks. Geez, she was acting like something out of *Love Comics*. Josh pulled off his cap and slipped it over her head. "So long, Birdie." He shoved his boat off the sand. Dancing like a clown as the water spilled into his tennis shoes, he jumped into the bow.

She waded out into the water. Oh, Josh. Don't leave. He started the motor and jerked the gearshift into forward. Slowly, she raised her arm and waved good-bye.

For a moment, he turned away, fumbling. When he faced her again, both of his arms were draped over his head. There was a third arm on the throttle. The fake one. "Look, no hands!" he called as he slipped away across the rippling waters of Whitefish Lake.